THE
HAWK'S
TALE

ALSO BY JOHN BALABAN

POETRY

After Our War

Blue Mountain

FICTION

Coming Down Again

TRANSLATION

Caa Dao Vietnam:

A Bilingual Anthology of

Vietnamese Folk Poetry

THE
HAWK'S
TALE

by

JOHN
BALABAN

illustrated by

DAVID DELAMARE

GULLIVER BOOKS

HARCOURT BRACE JOVANOVICH

San Diego   Austin   Orlando

HBJ

Requests for permission to make copies of any
part of the work should be mailed to:
Permissions, Harcourt Brace Jovanovich, Publishers,
Orlando, Florida 32887.

Library of Congress Cataloging-in-Publication Data
Balaban, John, 1943–   The hawk's tale.
Summary: Follows the adventures of a toad, a mouse,
and a young water snake as they set out to rescue the
mouse's niece who was carried off by a hawk and
encounter their powerful ruler, the White Eagle.
[1. Animals—Fiction. 2. Fantasy] I. Title.
PZ7.B1794Haw 1988   [Fic]   87-14938
ISBN 0-15-200462-9
Designed by Camilla Filancia
Printed in the United States of America
First edition
A B C D E

For my daughter, Tally

TABLE OF CONTENTS

vi

THE
HAWK'S
TALE

O N E

A Certain Snake Learns about a Shell,

Which Never Belonged to Any Turtle

Deep in the heart of the great forest, Glister said to Mirais, "Gosh, it's a dull day." Glister was a snake, a little water snake, and Mirais was an old, very large toad, a very large and very wise toad, so all the pond-folk said.

"Oh, but I agree," replied the toad, who had been dozing by the water's edge on a smooth stone that the sun had warmed. "I do agree."

"The Pond has sunk almost to nothing. Where once I used to swim, I now have to wriggle across weasel tracks and raccoon tracks and muskrat tracks, even possum tracks, and such," the little snake complained.

1

"It *is* getting dangerous with so little water in the Pond."

"Yes, there was Lilac last—" Glister stopped, remembering that Mirais had been fond of Lilac. Glister said no more about her. "The days are dull and the nights are dangerous," he sighed. "And there's nothing to do!"

"Well, that's true," said Mirais as he rubbed his forehead, on which shone the emerald jewel that all toads have. He was an old toad and it was a large jewel. "For good luck," he said, while rubbing his green jewel and looking down at Glister, who was floating in the still water.

Glister, his head all sticky with duckweed and water grass, wriggled up the bank to where Mirais sat on the smooth stone. The snake slipped up beside the toad, leaving a curvy wet track on the dry, dusty surface of the rock. If he had been an older snake, or just any snake, Mirais certainly would never have bothered with him, but Glister came from a family of snakes known both for their bravery and their thoughtfulness to the pondfolk. Shaking off a streamer of water fennel, Glister asked if Mirais had yet had his dinner.

Mirais could see that Glister was itching to do something. Although the toad felt like doing nothing more than basking in the sun and listening to the crickets, he said, "Glister, my friend, do you think you would be content to rest a while—especially if I told a story?"

"Oh. Oh, yes," said Glister, though really he had hoped for a race across the Pond, or something a bit more exciting. He noticed that the little peepers were croaking again now that he had glided past them. Though he was only a little snake, he thought, just the same the little frogs had hidden from him as he swam by. Oh, but he was proud, as a young snake will often be. Glister coiled on the sunny rock, puffed himself, and looked very pleased. In the cool bushes crickets sang.

"Considering that young weasels get similar respect from certain water reptiles," said the toad, truly reading Glister's thoughts, "I wouldn't make too much of the little frogs' fear."

"Oh, yes, but—"

"But don't we know what a shameful kind of respect fear is?"

"Yes, Mirais, but—"

Ploosh! Something hit the water.

A bullfrog had dived to escape a hawk. When Glister heard the dive and caught sight of a dark fan of wings sailing low, he darted under the rock on which he had been resting. But Mirais had not moved. "See what I mean, snake?" he croaked down from the top of the stone.

Glister wondered how the toad knew just when to jump and when to sit. He admired the toad. For didn't the toad's very age prove his wisdom? There was no other toad in the Pond who was so right as Mirais, nor so old.

As Glister slithered back onto the rock, he saw the toad studying his reflection in the clear water where the bullfrog had broken the Pond's green film. The toad looked thoughtfully and very deeply into the water. Glister knew that Mirais was thinking of a good story.

High above, locusts were singing in the trees that ringed the sleepy Pond. Now and then, the snake heard a thrush turning over dry leaves in the bushes by the edge of the forest. After a while the toad looked up from the water into which he had been looking and turned to Glister.

"Friend snake," he said, "what do you think is the strongest animal in the world?" Mirais cocked an eye and studied his companion.

"Oh, that's very easy. A bear, or maybe a wildcat."

"Bear! Hah. 'A bear,' he says."

"Well, then, a mountain lion," said Glister, a little embarrassed.

"No, Glister. It is clear you have never heard of what lies beyond the deep woods."

Mirais was right. *Beyond* the deep woods! Why, the snake had never even been *in* the deep woods that ringed the Pond. It was a fearful place. Not a place for a little water snake. There was a brook that flowed quickly from the Pond, trickling over the mossy rocks where crayfish and minnows and salamanders and water bugs made their homes. His uncle, Alcor, who was a daring fellow and a brawny blacksnake, had traveled down the cool, shady brook to see what was in the deep forest. Years later he had come back—oh, gosh—telling the pondfolk of unheard-of things: of where the water dropped through the air in a big roar, of great rivers, and of huge fish with golden scales. Alcor had left again (years ago, before Glister was born) to search even farther. Another uncle, a grass snake, Mizar, had gone along too. Glister's mother had said they joked and swam on their backs when they left. They never came back.

"Friend, what's wrong?" said Mirais, who saw the snake's sad look.

"It's my two uncles," said Glister forlornly. "They must have been eaten by a bear or a bobcat."

"Now, what a silly thought. What a silly thought, indeed."

"Why?" said Glister, taking his head out of his coiled tail and looking up hopefully, even if a bit tearfully.

"Bears and bobcats are as big as the trees. They don't bother with little snakes. How do I know? Why, I've seen them—but they didn't see me."

"Really, you've seen bears and lions? Where?"

"In the woods near here, but in the winter when most everybody is asleep. Even bears sleep, you know."

"Have you really been to the deep woods?" said Glister.

"Indeed, I have, snake. Indeed, I have."

Glister stared in awe.

"Come on, let's go to Duck Hill," said Mirais,

hopping down from the rock. "There we can sit and see where the brook runs into the forest."

"Let's go!" said Glister, winding swiftly along the grassy path.

"There I'll tell you about the strongest animal," said the toad, huffing as he slowly hopped along, "for it is not even the bear."

As the old toad and the young snake made their way up the dusty bank where Duck Hill sloped steeply down to the Pond, they saw two blue jays—well-known troublemakers—swooping and shrilling at something lying on the top of the hill.

"Bah! Those no-good jays," said Mirais.

"What have they got?" asked Glister, who was having difficulty getting up the steep, dusty bank and was too low to the ground to see well.

"Oh, they are playing pranks on some poor box turtle who has shut himself up in his shell."

The birds raised a racket that shattered the quiet of the Pond. Flapping above the shell, they paid no attention to the toad and the snake as the two reached the crest of the hill.

"Oo-er, this *is* a hard shell," said one bird, pecking at the top.

"Sounds empty," said the other.

"Sounds like the joke is on you," said Mirais, hopping closer. For now Mirais saw something that the blue jays did not.

"Well, wise toad, what do you say? What's the matter with this turtle?" said one jay.

"Why is his shell so hard?" said the other.

Mirais winked at the snake, who was blinking with the dust raised by the blue jays. "By my jewel, my feathered friends," Mirais began, "that shell does not, nor ever did, belong to any turtle."

That stopped the birds' railing.

"What?" they cried in one voice. "Never belonged to any turtle?"

"No turtle."

The jays walked curiously around the dark hump, pecking, trying to turn it over. It was too heavy and deep in the grass. "It looks like a turtle," they said.

"Did it poke its head, or arms, or legs out?" asked the snake.

"No, and he was all covered with grass when we spied him."

"Blue jays, if you want you may hear a story, which I was just about to tell Glister,

Which story, I think,
If you listen well,
Will explain the mystery
Of this turtle shell,
Which never belonged to any turtle."

Mirais smiled broadly at the snake. The jays flew up to sit on a low twisting branch spreading from the old oak, which grew at the top of Duck Hill.

One of the jays answered:

7

"Let's hear your tale, bejeweled Mirais,
But don't be so awfully pious.
We're beautiful and busy jays
And simply haven't got all day."

"Very good, jay! Very good, indeed." Mirais was delighted with such clever company, even if they were rude blue jays. "The story goes like this: Many years ago, more than our oldest grandparents can remember, there lived in the world an animal smarter and fiercer than the bear, the bobcat, and the fox all in one." Mirais turned to Glister, who had curled in the grass by the shell on which the toad sat. As he talked, crickets sang in the cool shadows. "His name was Man . . ."

"Man," repeated the jays and the snake in one voice.

". . . and he lived so long ago that not even the owl's grandfather, with whom I have often spoke of this, remembers seeing him."

"What about the shell?" said the jays up on the branch. "Did Man move like a turtle?"

"No. This Man was almost as big as the bear. He stood straight up on his back legs, and was so clever as to rule all the animals in the forest. He made some of them work for him. Yet he did not live in the forest, nor do I know where he lived. All this I was told by my great-grandfather, Darius, who was the wisest of all toads, God rest his soul. For all I know, Man may

8

still live somewhere, but certainly he has never come again to the forest."

Just then—almost before his last words were out— the grass began to shake around the bottom of the shell on which Mirais was sitting.

The jays flew up shrieking.

Mirais hopped from the trembling shell.

Glister hid under an oak root.

The grass around the shell quivered. Mirais watched the shell. Pretty soon a little pink nose poked out from under it. Then some whiskers. Then the whole head. "What's all this talk about my house?" said an angry little voice.

It was a mouse. A mouse with eyeglasses. The blue jays flew back down to their perch; Glister crept out from the root. Mirais just sat looking at the little fellow. All were embarrassed—except the mouse, of course.

"I'll finish the story, if you please," said the toad somewhat huffily. Still, he was intrigued by this rather strange mouse.

"Mr. Trembly is the name," said the mouse.

"Well, Mr. Trembly, I was just telling my friends the story of your house." Mirais now recognized Mr. Trembly as one of the deer mice who kept to themselves at the edge of the Pond.

"Are *these* your friends?" The mouse pointed angrily to the jays, who were pretending to look the other way. "Well, go on," the mouse said. "I heard the beginning, I may as well listen to the end." Mr. Trembly scratched his whiskers and made himself comfortable on the twisted knob of an old bare root.

Mirais climbed back onto the shell and cleared his throat. Then he rubbed the bright, shining jewel on his forehead. He smiled to his audience: the jays on the branch, the snake in the grass, and the bold little mouse with black, shiny eyes and wire-rimmed spectacles.

> *"Friends, if you listen well,*
> *You'll know the secret of the shell,*
> *Which belongs to this mouse,*
> *As, indeed, it is his house."*

Mirais winked at the blue jay who had rhymed before. From where he sat, Mirais could see the entire pond. The afternoon was very quiet. Crickets and locusts and little peepers sang along the edge of the green, still water. A hummingbird flew slowly from poppy to red poppy at the boggy end of the far side. Behind him, the toad could hear the creek tinkling like a flood of little bells over the mossy rocks as it disappeared into the deep woods.

"When Man came to the deep woods, all animals fled in fear of him." Mirais looked sharply at Glister. "Men—that's the plural, you know—killed many animals, even the bear, so that all animals hated men. Often the men made the trees burn, leaving many animals without homes. Flames as tall as trees devoured the forest. One day men entered the woods in great numbers and began to fight among themselves. They fought, not singly as animals do, but in herds. They stayed for a long, long time. The woods were burnt black. The trees were charred and splintered as if by lightning. Smoke filled the air. Dead animals and dead men and the things they carried littered the ground and choked the streams. Then, after a while, the noise grew less. The men grew fewer. Soon there were no more men in the forest. Darius, my great-grandfather, said that his great-grandfather saw men covering their heads with hard shells like this." Mirais tapped the shell with his foot.

"Ah-hah! That explains why the shell never moved," said one blue jay.

"And why it lay so deep in the grass," said the other.

"And why I did not know the name of the strongest animal," said Glister, the young green snake who liked the summer water and adventure.

11

T W O

They Begin Their Quest

"Toad, tell me," said the little brown mouse, "how is it known that the world is now empty of men?"

"Truthfully, Mr. Trembly, I do not know. But some years past I myself made a trip into the woods and none of the forest folk then had heard of them."

"My uncle, Alcor, did not mention them either," said Glister, turning in a slow S around a dry tree root, which had arched free of the earth.

"How would you like to make a trip into the forest to find out?" Mr. Trembly asked.

"Count us out!" cried the blue jays.

"Count me in!" said Glister.

"What about you, Mirais?" asked the mouse.

"What for, Mr. Trembly? What good would it do to know? No, I don't think so. I don't think so. Just to find adventure?"

"Well, to tell the truth, I would be looking for something else, something which I lost only a few days ago," said the mouse.

"Oh?" said Mirais.

"My niece, Lilac," replied the mouse. He trembled and pulled nervously at the cuff of his sleeve.

"By my jewel! By my jewel!"

"Lilac! Was she your niece?" asked Glister.

"She *is* my niece."

"Where *is* she, then?" asked the two blue jays.

"Somewhere in the forest."

"How do you know?" asked Glister.

"A friend of mine, a water rat, came to tell me late one night of a rumor he had heard from a muskrat who lives by the brook. The muskrat told of a young mouse who was being kept by a family of muskrats very deep in the forest."

"And how did she get there?" asked Mirais, who had been much devoted to this little niece of Mr. Trembly. Lilac wasn't like the other deer mice, who were very shy and cared only about gathering dandelion seeds and strawberries for themselves. No, Lilac worried about other creatures besides herself. Mirais remembered how she had carried a blackberry every day to Felix, the crippled cricket who hurt his leg and couldn't sing or hop and who was very sad.

"The water rat said a hawk snatched and carried her off . . ."

"I thought as much," said the toad. Probably, he thought, she had been caught out in the open on the way to see Felix.

". . . and dropped her by accident over the depths of the woods."

"Well, no more talk, friend mouse. You're going, and Glister and I are going with you. Right, Glister?"

"Oh, yes, sir," said the snake, rolling over with excitement.

Two days later, carrying backpacks (woven from dried grass by Mildred, Mr. Trembly's wife), the toad, the mouse, and the snake hiked along the creek that flowed into the dark forest from Duck Pond. The creek water licked the mossy bank and sometimes kicked up cool spray around their feet. They listened to the music of the clear water and marched along—the old toad first—intending to travel down the creek until they found the muskrat who had told the water rat the rumor of the lost Lilac. Then they would decide whether his tale were true or not and whether to go on. That was their plan. They hiked in silence, each thinking his own thoughts.

Glister was sad as he followed Mirais. Glister had never been away from home before. That morning when the pondfolk had gathered at the bottom of Duck Hill to say good-bye, Glister's mother had cried so hard she almost made him cry. "Now, now," his father had said, "he's in good hands with the toad, and that mouse is no fool either." But Glister's mother had just cried some more. And now, winding through the strange dark forest, Glister felt lonely and far away from his friends. But, gosh, he thought, suddenly feeling brave again, this was an *adventure*, a *real* adventure, not just a race across the sleepy Pond or teasing a mean raccoon. With that, Glister zipped around the toad and took the lead through a thicket of ferns.

Mr. Trembly followed last, wiping the water spray from his eyeglasses with a little white handkerchief embroidered in one corner with a blue letter T. *Oh, Lilac*, he sighed. Poor Lilac. It was his fault. All his fault. When Lilac's parents were swept away by a flash flood years ago, he and Mrs. Trembly had tried to raise little Lilac as if she were one of their own many children. But she was always different. He cautioned her to be careful like the other mice, but Lilac was too full of fun and too worried about others to heed his warnings. Now what was a mouse doing helping a cricket? But that was Lilac. Mr. Trembly also remembered how she had once sailed across Duck Pond in a little jack-in-the-pulpit boat that the wind twirled around in the water and nearly tipped over. Who ever heard of a mouse on the water? But that was little Lilac. Mr. Trembly plodded along with a heavy heart, adjusting his rain cap and shifting the weight of his backpack and his acorn canteen. A big red feather stuck out from his pack like a flag. Mr. Trembly's white paws looked like gloves, and in the right paw he grasped a stick for testing slippery rocks at creek crossings. All his life he had kept to himself and out of trouble, as a mouse properly should, and now . . . *Oh, Lilac,* he thought, and plodded on after the toad.

Old Mirais was in good spirits. He hopped on ahead through the fiddlehead ferns with a spring in his old flippity-flop, as he called it. He was remembering how the jays had brought together all the pondfolk for a good-bye. Mirais thought there wasn't a bad apple in the bunch: fat robins and noisy sparrows, bullfrogs, peepers, and wiggly tadpoles with their eyes poked just above the water. The muskrats with muddy paws, were lined up on the bank, along with rabbits from the clover patch and the shrews that lived under logs. The box turtles lumbered out of the skunk cabbage swamp, one chipmunk kept squeaking with excitement, and even the grouchy old snapping turtle that nobody had seen for weeks rose right up from the bottom of the Pond—muck all over him—to say good-bye with a big yawn of his sharp, crooked jaws. And there were all of Mirais's cousins sitting on top of the hollow, half-sunken log that was his home. Why, when the sunlight struck the log and the congregation of toads, all their jeweled foreheads gathered an emerald light that made the whole log glow green. It was a good sign. Not, of course, as good a sign as the red cardinal's feather that the mouse had found lying on the roof of his house that morning. That was really a sign of good luck and bon voyage, for the cardinal wasn't just a bird, but a messenger of magic. Some folk even said that the cardinal was sent by the White Eagle that ruled the forest and Pond. Oh, surely, Mirais thought as he sniffed the air and felt young again, surely they would find Lilac and save her from the cruel creatures of the woods. And along the way, the old toad thought, he would teach young Glister the ways of the world. Yes, and help poor, worried, and brave Mr. Trembly learn the joys of adventure and of meeting new folk.

"Hello!" yelled Mirais at a turtle perched on a mossy rock in the middle of the stream. "HAL-LO-OO," he called again even louder, but the rush of the water drowned out the toad's call so the turtle could not hear them. He only waved and stared in curiosity at the three moving along the bank heading deeper into the forest: the quick snake sliding through the fern bank, the big old toad hopping along and waving back, and the nearsighted mouse testing his route with a walking stick.

THREE

The Writer Tells How
He Learned This Tale

I heard it from a crow who learned it from a hawk.
How the hawk learned this tale I do not know, but
in the dense forest many strange things happen. As
I think that the journey of Mirais, Glister, and Mr.
Trembly in search of Lilac was closely watched by the
more magical folk of the forest, it is enough to say
that, usually, the owl and, always, the cardinal know
all that goes on in the deep woods: from underneath
the rustling, dead leaves on the forest floor to the
highest branches of the oaks, rocking in the wind.
Now *how* I heard it from a crow is *my* secret.

FOUR

In Which the Mouse Is Taught to Row
and the Snake Learns to Watch
with His Ears

Many warm days and chilly nights passed and still the toad, the snake, and the mouse trudged on along the brook's green, winding bank. Now evening was creeping across the floor of the forest. The woods were getting dark and misty with the damp air that rose from the wet places where the ferns and mosses grew. As the sun set far out of sight, its last light hung in the tallest branches of the hemlocks far above the travelers' heads. Soon, even the topmost branches were dark and it was black but for the cold moonlight and the flickerings of the fireflies. The three dropped their backpacks and rested on the soft, spongy moss.

"How much farther will we go?" asked Glister, who was tired and a little frightened of the dark.

Mirais and Mr. Trembly looked at each other.

"Till we find Lilac," said Mirais. "Until we find Lilac."

Of all the animals they had asked, not one, so far, had given them any real help. Some said to search farther downstream for the muskrats that might be taking care of Lilac. And so they had searched farther, day after day, poking their heads down rabbit holes among the twisted roots of trees; hallooing down muskrat burrows dug into the wet banks of the brook. All with no luck.

"She may be dead," said Mr. Trembly, trying to sound matter-of-fact, but giving himself away by darting his little black eyes not toward Mirais, to whom he was speaking, but toward his own feet. "I do not think we should search much longer. The summer, you know, is almost over."

He was right. Though the days seemed long with searching, they were really much shorter. The nights were cold. The leaves—the sycamore's first, then the walnut's—were already starting to turn color. As it would soon be time to prepare for the long sleep that silenced the whole woods in winter, something had to be done quickly.

Glister thought of the rocky den where soon his whole family would curl together until springtime.

Mirais, rubbing his forehead, thought of his warm, hollow log by the edge of the Pond.

Mr. Trembly, poor fellow, thought only of his little niece lost somewhere in the great, dark woods where the hawk's talons, the bobcat's claws, and the drowning water were always hungry for a little deer mouse. Even if she were safe in a muskrat's house, how could she stand the winter in a wet, cold, watery place? Lilac was used to other mice, to featherdown, and to soft, dry straw in their snug shell house.

Sadly the weary three listened silently to the water rushing past them. Moonlight danced on the surface of the brook. The crickets sang. Bullfrogs croaked. An owl hooted.

"Hey, mates! Why so sad? Ahoy!"

All three squinted toward the water.

"Who-o-o's there?" stuttered Glister.

"Where are you?" asked Mr. Trembly, brandishing his walking stick.

"What do you want?" demanded the toad.

"Is you the three mates that's been looking for a little mouse?" was all their answer. They heard a splash. Dimly, they could see a little boat making for shore. A firefly lamp swung from a spar, faintly lighting the half-deck. As the little boat rowed closer to the bank, they could make out wicker fishing baskets and nets on the deck, as well as the name *Water Skeeter* painted on the side. "If you be," continued the voice, which belonged to the dark rower guiding the boat to shore, "I say, if you be, I might just be able to help you."

"We are indeed looking for a mouse," said Mirais. "The niece of my associate here, Mr. Trembly." Mr.

Trembly smiled hopefully at the figure in the boat, who on closer inspection appeared to be an old musk-rat with shaggy gray whiskers and a wrinkled nose and black eyes that winked in the firefly light. He had on baggy gray trousers, a rough, old blue sweater, and a sea captain's cap.

"This is Glister," continued the toad, "and I'm called Mirais."

"Pleased to meet you. Pelagon, Cap'n Pelagon's my name."

"Do—" began the mouse.

"Just a moment, and I'll come ashore." In two shakes, he docked his boat. "Been looking for you fellows all day," said he as he shook Mirais's hand. "I brought me boat up into these narrows when I heard about you fellows this morning." Mr. Trembly and Glister both then noticed a small red feather tucked into the Captain's cap. Mirais caught their look, smiled broadly, rubbed his jewel, and invited the Captain to sit down. "Never made a more keel-crackin', sand-scrapin' run in all me life than in these shallows!" finished the Captain, tugging up his worn trousers at the knee as he sat down on a log.

"Do you know where Lilac is?" asked Mr. Trembly.

"Who?" said the Captain.

"The little mouse," said Mirais.

"Oh, aye. The little mouse. Well, I may and I may not. What with all the stops I make along this water," said the Captain, pointing downstream, "I did hear of a little mouse way downriver. But whether she's your Like-a-lot—"

"Lilac," said Glister.

"—your Leelac, I can't say, but I figure you'll get farther and get there faster with me than on foot, so you're welcome to come aboard and take the trip downstream with ol' Pelagon."

"We certainly will," said Mirais, "if it's no trouble to you." Mirais had a feeling that this meeting was no accident.

"Can you travel at night?" asked the Captain.

"Sure can."

"Well, mates, then toss your packs over the port bow and climb aboard!"

Glister and Mirais scrambled on board, but Mr. Trembly hesitated, looking fearfully at the dark, swift water.

"Jump, mate!" said Captain Pelagon. "We're not a rat's whisker away from shore."

"Jump, Mr. Trembly, we'll catch you," said the snake, who was curled about the rail.

The mouse trembled, looking around the bank uncertainly. Then he took five steps back, adjusted his pack, cap, stick, and spectacles, and made a running leap at the boat and . . . PLOOSH!

"Mouse overboard!" roared the Captain. The three on board reached down for the mouse struggling in the cold, churning water. The Captain stopped him with an oar. Glister anchored his tail about the mouse's arm. And Mirais grabbed him by the scruff of the neck. All three gave one pull and . . . landed the shivering mouse on the deck.

"Cast off, snake," bellowed the Captain. Glister darted to the rail and freed the mooring line. "Throw a blanket around that mouse, toad." Mirais pulled one out from under the half-deck. "Hey, mate. Trembly, there! Bite down on those teeth before they rattle out of your jaws." The Captain laughed, slapped the shivering mouse on the back, and began to row.

"Glister, me lad," he said, "we're headed out to midstream. It's too shallow here for the sail. You watch at the bow for rocks, logs—anything up in the water."

"But it is dark, sir. How can I see?" asked the little snake.

"Well, lad, you watch with your . . . uh . . . your ears. Listen for fast water. If you hear a gurgling or a fast rush, that means something's breaking the surface. Then you sing out. Can you do it?" The snake shook his head eagerly. "Good lad."

"What can I help with?" asked Mirais.

"Well, mate, and no offense, but you're a bit old for learning to row. Now rowing will keep the mouse warm. We'll put him on the oars when we reach clearer water. But, for now, you two get your rest. After that, matey, you take the snake's watch." Mirais objected but saw the truth in what Pelagon had said.

The Captain dug a pipe out of a pocket, lit it, blew

a puff of sweet-smelling blue smoke, and leaned back on the oars.

The night wore on. The moon, which had risen high, shimmered on the water. Mr. Trembly and Mirais slept under blankets. All that could be heard was the occasional hoot of an owl, the lap of the water, the creak of the deck, and the splash of the Captain's oars. Even the frogs were quiet. After a while the Captain woke Mr. Trembly and showed him how to row. Glister listened closely for dangerous water.

When even the fireflies went to sleep, the Captain lighted a grass lamp and hung it from the sail-shrouded mast. Then, walking to a chest, he took out a small mandolin. Seated under the dim light, leaning against the mast, he began to play. The Captain sang in a rough, quiet way, and the old toad woke from his sleep to listen.

> "If you're from way downriver
> Where the salt sinks in the mud
> Or where lizards climb the ledges
> For to warm their springtime blood,
> You've heard no doubt of Pelagon
> And his boat, the Water Skeeter,
> For of all the tradin' craft afloat
> There's none on the River to beat her.
>
> I've sailed this river thirty years
> From the shallows to the bay.

If ever you had some goods to haul
Anywhere on the water's way,
You've heard no doubt of Pelagon
And his boat, the Water Skeeter,
For of all the tradin' craft afloat
There's none on the River to beat her.

I tried every rocky inlet
And tacked every sandy shore.
My guess is that they'll be saying
For another thirty or more:
You've heard no doubt of Pelagon
And his boat, the Water Skeeter,
For of all the tradin' craft afloat
There's none on the River to beat her."

When the Captain finished his song, he stood up, coughed, knocked the dead ashes from his pipe, and returned the mandolin to the chest. Then, taking over the oars from Mr. Trembly, he rowed the boat into quiet water in the lee of a wooded island where an owl was hooting softly in a dead tree that hung over the foggy stream. "Drop anchor, snake," whispered the Captain, "and drop 'er quiet-like." He gave a nod toward the dead tree silhouetted against the moon. "Mr. Toad," he said, "you tuckered out or just thinking?"

Wrapped snug in a blanket to keep the damp air from his old bones, the toad sat with his back against

an aft rail. "Both, Captain. Both," was all the toad said as he watched the moon sailing high above them. Sleepy old toad, he watched and listened to water churning in an eddy, to waves slapping gently at the sides of the boat as it rocked and creaked on its anchor rope. He was thinking of how far they had come and of how far they might have to go to find unlucky Lilac. As the toad drifted off to sleep, he heard the owl hoot again and he almost thought he heard Lilac's playful squeak somewhere in the dark woods.

"Well, mates," said the Captain, pulling a blanket out for himself and looking at his weary crew, "turn in. We're out of the worst water and nary a snag. Tomorry, we'll try the main sail. Now, bundle up and don't roll overboard." The Captain laughed as he blew out the lamp. "Aye, mate," he said to the old toad, "it's a rum go at our age."

"Hoo-hoo. Hoo-hoo-hoo."

They all tugged their blankets up to their chins, except for Glister, who had coiled entirely under his.

Soon the old muskrat captain began to snore.

"Hoo?" cried the owl looking for prey.

Overhead, above the anchored boat and above the perched owl—overhead, above the trees—the moon and the planets and a sprinkle of stars winked through the swirling mists as the boat rocked its crew to sleep.

FIVE

A Dangerous Adventure
and a Watery Grave

When Mirais awoke in the morning, his old eyes discovered a sight they had never seen before: the River—not a small stream, but the River. It was broad and swift and seemed to be shallow. It was more green than blue and more brown than green. The sun danced brightly on its surface where the water broke about an island or a rock. Dark green trees crowded its edge. Wooded islands dotted the horizon like distant ships at anchor. In the sandy shallows by the shore, large, stilt-legged birds fished for minnows. Not far from where the *Water Skeeter* lay, huge fish with golden scales—bigger fish than Mirais had ever seen—rolled in the sun.

"Carp," said Captain Pelagon, who had just awakened.

"Carp," said Mirais as he shook the snake and the mouse to see the sight.

"Captain, I say, Captain, do you ever fish for fish like these?" asked the toad. His back ached from sleeping on a pile of ropes.

"Not me. I never fish at all. This here is a tradin' boat. Me father was a fisherman. It's not for me."

After breakfast they weighed anchor and set sail. The Captain held the tiller and trimmed the sail. Mr. Trembly and Glister sat at the bow squinting at the broad, shining river. Mirais sat near the tiller talking with the Captain.

That day and many others ran by like warm water sliding past the bow. The new sights were endless: deer drinking carefully by the shore, ducks landing noisily at dusk, otters chasing one another. Glister once spotted a large moose rising from feeding on the river's bottom grasses—a dripping, yellow crown of water fennel wreathed about his rack, water streaming from his muddy chin. Gosh, what an adventure! Glister couldn't wait to tell them all back home.

Soon they noticed autumn leaves drifting downstream in bright reds and yellows. One afternoon, the Captain said that in less than two days they would reach the muskrat village where Lilac might be. It was just then that the toad, the mouse, and the snake learned of the danger that lay ahead.

"What is that humming sound?" asked Glister. He looked nervously downstream.

"Yes, what is it, Captain? I have been hearing it for a half hour," said Mr. Trembly. Mirais listened, but heard nothing.

"Your ears are younger than mine, mates. You've caught the sound mine have been listening for all morning."

"What is that, Captain? What sound is that?" asked old Mirais, whose hearing was no longer sharp either.

"Well, mates, it's the Falls. It takes some doing to get around her, and for more reasons than one. Now, this boat would be smashed to smithereens if we went over."

"Can't we carry her down the banks?" asked Mirais.

"But for one thing, and here's where you may decide to go it on foot again. And I wouldn't be blaming you if you did."

"What's that?" Mr. Trembly asked, looking up from sewing a patch on an old sail.

"Bears, mate. They fish the rapids below the Falls."

"Are they far from here?" asked Glister with a worried look.

"How do we get around them?" asked Mirais.

"We—that is, if you're game—we don't go around them, we go *under* them," said the Captain. He pointed to the far bank. "In there," he said, "is cut a long, spiraling channel. The muskrats cut 'er long ago. She's cut just so," he said, making a large O with his hands. You rush down with only a rat's tail of air whisking above your mast. You go down fast, aye, with neither tiller nor oar. In the spring she's too full to run, 'cause them what's tried have lost their boats. If you make it"—Glister looked ahead uneasily—"you come out below the rapids in the slow water. Are you game?"

The three looked at each other.

"We're game," said Mirais.

In a little while they reached the far bank. The Captain guided the boat along the bank so as not to rush past the channel opening. The water began to run faster. The roar of crashing waves was getting louder. Then Glister spotted the Falls by the white spray billowing above the surface of the River, just a little downstream.

"Steady as she goes. There's our channel." Now the toad, the snake, and the mouse saw a dark hole in the bank. Black and wide, it yawned open, gulping down water like the mouth of a huge, hungry fish. "Mirais, you sit in the stern with me." The Captain pointed to the snake and the mouse. "You two sit down on either side of the mast. Everybody grab hold! We're going down!" roared the Captain.

As the bow caught the channel current, the mast brushed the vines hanging over the lip of the tunnel. The boat held poised for one second, and then pitched down into darkness. The water roared in their ears. "Hold on!" yelled the Captain. The smooth mud walls rushed by. "Hold on!" he yelled again, but they could barely hear him as the rush of the surging water drowned out his voice. Faster and faster they shot forward, downward, down in a circle.

Not too long, however, and the water slowed.

"We're comin' to the cavern!" shouted Captain Pelagon. No sooner had he spoken than the boat entered slower water. A broad section had been cut in the channel to slow down the race of the water. The boat was now well inside the hill by the right of the Falls.

The Captain struck a light.

All gave a fearful shudder. The shores of the small cavern in which they drifted were choked with the hulls of wrecked boats. The muddy bones of the drowned sailors moldered among rotting, splintered planking. Slowly, they drifted through the ghastly cavern until again the water roared ahead.

The Captain blew out the light.

"Hold on, mates! There's one last run!" As he shouted, the boat dipped down and spun into the racing water. Suddenly, the boat turned about. The water battered her side.

"Lean on the tiller!" Pelagon shouted.

"The tiller!" shouted Mirais, giving his weight to it, too. The force of the water flung the Captain and Mirais back. The tiller swung wild. The boat began to shake and roll. Then Glister and Mr. Trembly scurried back to help. They leaned hard with the other two to straighten the boat, bow first. Slowly they forced the tiller to turn the boat around. Then, with a crack, the tiller broke off in their hands, but the boat, turned right again, shot forward like a cork. Spiraling down and down, down and down—crunching, grinding, scraping past the narrow walls. Bobbing in the black tunnel. Flooded with spray, the boat lurched forward.

"There's a light ahead," yelled Glister.

"We made it!" shouted the mouse. The boat glided out into clear, sunny water. "We made it!" shouted the mouse once more, but in back of them came a great, ferocious, angry roar.

"Bear! Raise that sail!" Mr. Trembly jumped to at the Captain's orders. The mouse and the snake began to hoist the sail.

"Hurry," cried Mirais, hopping up and down. "He's gaining; he's almost on us!"

Roaring and crashing, the bear lunged after them from across the rocky shore where it had been fishing below the rapids. But the bear was too late. Using an oar for a rudder, the Captain sailed the boat into clear, deep water. Behind them, raking and slashing the water angrily with his claws, the bear fumbled in the deep river while Mr. Trembly and the snake laughed.

"By my jewel, what is that over there, Captain?" asked Mirais. He stared ahead across the water.

"That, mate, is the muskrat village."

A long, grassy bank on the left side of the River

was all riddled with burrows. Boats lay quietly at the dock in front of the village. Mirais looked thoughtfully at Mr. Trembly.

"Haul out your mandolin, Pelagon," he said, "and I'll add a verse or two to your song."

"Right, mate." The Captain went to the chest. "Just give me some time to shake out the water. Mouse, you trim the sail. Snake, you watch at the bow. We'll take her in in style."

The Captain plucked the tune, and old Mirais rubbed his forehead and croaked out some more lines to the Captain's song:

> *"Don't tell me of your risky runs*
> *Or scrapes along this water*
> *Until I sing of this fine boat and*
> *The danger through which we brought her.*
> *I sing this song of Pelagon*
> *And his boat, the* Water Skeeter,
> *For of all the tradin' craft afloat*
> *There's none on the River to beat her.*
>
> *We entered the muskrat channel*
> *Where water crashed the bow.*
> *We entered the black cavern*
> *That's choked with broken prows.*
> *We saw the bones all broken*
> *Like sticks along the shore*
> *And we left that deathly cavern*
> *To try our luck once more.*

Our boat reentered the channel;
She began to turn around
But Pelagon held the tiller
And kept her from running aground.
Though the water took our tiller
And split it with a shiver,
Another hour we shot straight out
Like a cork onto the River.

Then it was the bear came out,
Who thought we looked like dinner,
But the Water Skeeter took full sail—
At last we were the winner.
I'll sing this song of Pelagon
And his boat, the Water Skeeter,
For of all the tradin' craft afloat
There's none on the River to beat her."

As these last lines were sung, the *Water Skeeter* eased close to shore. All along the bank muskrats crowded to have a look. Some waved to Captain Pelagon and he waved back. Others dove into the water to swim about the boat. At last, the boat came to dock.

Of Events in the Land of Couronne,
in the Muskrat Village, and in
La Cheminée du Roi René

As Mr. Trembly, pushing his glasses up his long pink nose and standing in the bow of the *Water Skeeter*, squinted out at the muskrat village and beyond, he saw a scene which greatly pleased him. Behind the docks, which harbored many a smartly painted and trimly rigged ship, there was a long row—parallel to the bank—of houses thatched with cattail reeds. Each house, as he looked, was bathed in sunlight. Each had its own tunnel reaching to the water's edge. In front of each tunnel there was, stuck in the sand, a white sign painted with the name of the occupant in red letters: Abélard de Lune, Philippe Deschamps,

Jules Malfait, Marie Aiguille. Mr. Trembly scratched his neck where the wind had just ruffled his fur. The names sounded strange to him. Their strange sound and the tidy dooryards, about which grew plots of partridge peas, blue chicory, and pale blue gentian with its bottlelike blooms, reminded him of his own shell house and of how far he was from the Pond.

It certainly was a foreign land. Beyond the familiar pink knotweed and white-blossomed, leafy arrowhead plants growing by the water's edge, all was unfamiliar.

"My, what a strange and pleasant—what a strangely pleasant—sight," said Mr. Trembly to Mirais as the two looked out onto the long sloped fields kept by the muskrats.

"Do you think my uncles might have come this way?" asked the snake.

"We'll ask," said Mirais, remembering his own journey of long ago as he looked at the fields. Over there were soybeans all straightly furrowed. Farther, toward the distant edge of the forest, was a field of hay all neatly stacked in upright bundles. Wearing long white shirts and flailing long hand scythes, which glinted in the sunlight as they were swung, muskrats dotted the flat fields at the foot of the slopes. It was harvest time.

"What are those, Captain?" said Glister, pointing to many latticed red buildings brimming with yellow.

"Those be corncribs, skipper. Over there to the

41

starboard," he said, pointing to a field on the right, "where all those sheaves are being hauled in, is a cornfield." Mirais pointed at a cart, piled high with brown, strawlike stuff. "Buckwheat," said the Captain. "Wait till you have buckwheat muffins and cornbread, mouse," he said, with a wink to Mirais. "I warrant you'll find that a mite tastier than the sourdough and mulligan stew I've been dishing up."

Mr. Trembly remembered how the Captain had consoled him on the voyage with tales of the muskrat village. Now he could say he liked Coq d'Or (for that was its name) with all its neatness and busyness. Glister, hanging his head over the bow, liked it for its bright, shining water and shores. Mirais liked it for its order and for its settled look. And the Captain liked it. He liked it very much, he did, for there he had bought his first boat many years ago.

Mr. Trembly was reminded by the fading stalks of butterfly weed and by the dead leaves floating near the bank that fall was hard on them and that winter was not far behind. He saw goldenrod in an unplowed field. Surely, he thought, surely Lilac is here and soon we'll be home. Then I can say, he thought, that I've had a fine adventure, but that I will never leave the Pond again. The mouse looked hopefully at the crowd of nicely dressed muskrats jamming the dock. All were waiting to greet the voyagers as soon as Captain Pelagon moored his ship (which he then did), dropped anchor (which Glister and the mouse let go with a *kerplunk!*), and let down the gangplank (which, lastly, was done by the Captain). When the Captain led them down the gangplank, a chorus of shouts went up from the muskrats on the bank and from those crowding the dock.

"By my jewel," said Mirais, "these folks seem very friendly; they seem very friendly, indeed."

"Welcome back, Captain," said an old, bare-headed, white-haired muskrat in a long, purple robe that hung to his ankles and who held a sturdy staff of cedar in his right hand. "*Bonjour et bienvenue.*" The crowd hushed. Even the young muskrats bobbing in the water beside the *Water Skeeter* fell silent. "And welcome to your friends," he said, looking at Mr. Trembly, Mirais, and Glister, who each respectfully bowed low following the fashion of Captain Pelagon. "Welcome to Couronne, known in ancient times as Corona Hortuliani. *Pour vraiment,*" he said, sweeping his staff slowly toward the fields and meadows, "for truly, it is a 'crown garden.' Our village, Coq d'Or, welcomes you. *Je suis le Roi René.* That is to say, I am the King René and your ready servant." The King gave a nod with his head. Mirais and his two friends did the same. The little mouse's pink nose blushed with embarrassment, for neither he nor the snake knew what was the right thing to do or say.

But Mirais said, "We are awed by the beauty of Your Majesty's kingdom and humbled by your hospitality. My friends, Mr. Trembly"—the mouse smiled and, tucking his right arm over his belly and his left behind his back, gave a little bow; a chill breeze ruffled his fur—"and Glister"—who, being a snake had great difficulty with the civilities but managed a little, bobbing bow—"and myself, Mirais, are looking for the niece of my friend the mouse. Lilac's her name. She was, if we aren't mistaken, seized by a hawk and then dropped over the deep woods. We heard that she was alive and safe and here in the land of Couronne, to which Captain Pelagon has so kindly, so bravely, and so quickly guided us."

The King turned to the mouse. All the muskrats were very quiet. Some turned to each other and shook their heads. "Monsieur Trembly, your niece, I am afraid, is not here. However, she was until a few weeks ago. But, by Saint Bertilak, I assure you," said the King, "that she is safe and that you will be with her soon."

"But where is she?" said Mr. Trembly. Captain Pelagon lifted his cap and scratched his head. Mirais gravely watched the King. Glister, coiled on a pier butt, did too.

"*Allons*," said the King, lifting his staff. "Come, we shall talk at my house."

When he turned about, the crowd parted to let them pass. Many of those on the banks came to greet their old friend, the Captain, and to meet his friends.

"Mirais! Mirais!" shouted the Captain as he left a friend. "Tomorrow is the Harvest Day Celebration.

Wait till you see that, snake," he said to Glister, who was gliding behind them through the grass.

"What is it?" asked the snake.

The Captain lighted up a pipe. He winked at Mirais, hopping by his side. "You'll see tomorrow. Why, Trembly, star shooter that I've been for thirty years, by the dog, I must have lost track of the days. No idea it be so late."

Because each muskrat liked having a house near the water (a proverb in Couronne was "Live no farther from the water than its sound"), Coq d'Or (which, it seems, was the capital) was a long and narrow village. The muskrats lived in their houses only half the year— summer and fall. In the winter and springtime, they slept in their burrows underneath. They came up only for an occasional nibble at the grain stored dry above ground. Their houses were very much the same. King René's was the largest, but that was only because he was the village miller. His house was joined to a mill house that turned a large, wooden wheel with much rushing, scooping, dripping, and dropping of water all day and night of every day and night of the year, except when the millrace was frozen still. Glister thought the houses, near as they were to the water, were the most perfect houses he had ever seen. Mr. Trembly, though he was too polite to say so, found them cold and damp. Mirais thought them far too open above ground, remembering his warm log by the Pond. But the muskrats with their warm fur did not mind the cold and did not even think to chink the reed walls with mud and clay.

The King's house, because of the mill wheel, was slightly higher than the others and had a low porch. Red bergamot grew about it. Like the others, there was a white, red-lettered sign before the porch which read: *La Cheminée du Roi René*. Over the door was a stone lintel into which was cut the motto of the kingdom: MAIS IL FAUT CULTIVER NOTRE JARDIN (We must cultivate our garden).

The crowd waited while the King led Mirais, Mr. Trembly, Glister, and the Captain onto the porch. "Let each, *tout le monde*, remember his work and prepare for the holiday tomorrow," said the King to the muskrats before he dismissed them.

Sturdy wicker chairs were brought out onto the porch by the King's two grown sons, André and Claude. The brothers each tended an acre of land on the hillside by the forest, and, after introductions, they went out to their fields.

Before they sat down to talk, King René led the toad, the mouse, and the snake through his house. (Captain Pelagon found excuse to leave and visit with old friends.) It was a low, dark building, despite the many cracks of light shining through the breaks in the reed walls and the one large window in the slanted ceiling. Straw mats were spread on the dirt floor. There was a cherry wood cupboard, and a fine, round oak table upon which were set roughly carved wooden bowls, trenchers, cups, and spoons.

Down in the burrow beneath the house, the Queen was washing clothes over a washtub. The King laid his staff by the door and called down, "Hélène! Hélène! *S'il vous plaît.*" The sound of water sloshing in the washtub stopped. There was left only the sound of the water tinkling over the stone spillway leading to the river. "Hélène, come meet our guests, whom Captain Pelagon has brought."

"No, don't trouble her," insisted Mirais. "We'll go down."

A ladder stuck up out of the dark hole in the dirt floor. The King went first. Mirais next. Then Mr. Trembly. Then Glister, who twined himself down one side of the ladder. It was cold and dank in the tunnel, and slippery it was and dark. (Mr. Trembly wondered how they could like it *at all* down there and worried about slipping as he made a polite bow to the Queen.)

"Pleased to meet ya," said the Queen, somewhat roughly, strangling a shirt of the King's with one twist. The Queen did not stand on ceremony. "You go on up," she said. "I'll be up to fix you some nice herb tea and biscuits." But she was friendly. As Queen Hélène had soap up to her elbows and seemed more inclined to wash than to talk just then, the King and the three returned to the porch, leaving her humming a tune and sloshing sudsy water.

"Her Majesty is a simple woman," said the King a little stiffly, "and we are very busy getting ready, *très occupés*, for tomorrow." He adjusted his chair on the porch.

When Mirais and Mr. Trembly sat down (the snake found it easier to curl about in a porch pot containing some blue chicory), the King began: "Your account of Lilac's abduction is very accurate, Mirais. A family of squirrels from the forest brought her to us quite bruised and frightened. *En effet*, she had fallen, they said, right into their nest at the very top of an old oak tree. Getting her down was no easy matter, they said. *C'était fortune.* She stayed here until the weather turned colder, for then we feared that the damp nights by the river would be her finish, especially after so awful an experience. So we took her to the little girl, Molly."

"Little who?" asked the snake as he turned about a chicory stem.

"Little girl," said the King.

"What's a little girl?" asked the mouse. Even Mirais looked puzzled. But when the King described the size, shape, and nature of the little girl ("She's a very nice little girl," said the King, "and can, *vraiment*, do many things we muskrats can't do, and she is *toujours* willing to help us"), the toad smiled broadly. He rubbed the jewel on his forehead and reminded the little mouse and the water snake, who seemed much older than when they had started out, of the story of the shell, which never belonged to any turtle.

SEVEN

In Which Arrests Are Made, Justice Is Obtained,
and It Is Shown How There Are More Ways
Than One to Cultivate a Garden

As the old King and his guests from the distant pond
sat quietly talking on the porch, a burly, brawny, big,
rough-walking muskrat in a blue uniform with a little
silver star on his chest and carrying a club led two
muskrats—clearly farmers by their denim overalls—
before the King.

"Beggin' Your Majesty's worship," said the Sheriff
of Coq d'Or, for indeed it was he, "these men have
broken the law."

"What did they do?" said the King. He looked
sternly at them. In Couronne, one is guilty until proven
innocent. Glister's eyes widened and his tongue flicked

out nervously. The mouse looked at the toad, who asked the King if he thought they should leave for the moment.

"Stay," said the King. "Perhaps you can help."

The Sheriff looked surprised at that, but he continued in a loud voice, even a bit proudly. "These muskrats," pointing to the two (who looked very worried), "Cesar Paquerette and Philippe Vallon, farmers, are charged with breaking the most sacred laws of the realm: the abandoning of one's garden and the inciting of others to do the same. For with my own eyes, Your Highness . . . and, ah, Governors"—he so addressed the toad, the mouse, and the snake, since the King had made them part of the court—"I saw Philippe Vallon playing a guitar—"

"Which kind?" asked the King, now smiling broadly.

"Classical, Your Worship," said the Sheriff. "Take up the guitar and begin playing under an elm tree."

"You are certain that it was an elm?"

"Certain."

The Sheriff continued, looking a little confused at the King's question and the King's smile, "He, Philippe Vallon, thereby incited Cesar Paquerette to desert his bean patch and sit down under the elm where the aforementioned was playing." The Sheriff paused, flushed with the excitement of his duty.

"How do you plead?" asked the King.

"Guilty, Your Majesty," said the two sweat-stained farmers.

"Guilty to what?" said the King.

"To playing the guitar," said the one.

"To listening," said the other.

The King frowned at them. "Mirais, what do you think of this matter?"

"Well, Your Majesty, ah . . . really. I *am* a stranger in your land . . ."

"Why did you leave your plowing to play?" the King asked Vallon.

"Your Highness, a melody was in my head as I plowed, and I wanted to hear it."

"Why did you listen?"

"I liked his tune, Your Majesty."

"Sheriff," said the King, "we find these farmers not guilty of deserting their gardens." The Sheriff flushed red in the face. "Moreover, I fine you two bushels of soybeans for false accusation." The Sheriff shook with shame. "Mirais, tell me if you think the fine is just."

Mirais understood the King's meaning. "May I question the Sheriff, Your Majesty?" he asked.

"*Certainement.*"

"Sheriff, how did you first notice the playing?"

"I heard the tune as I was paddin' my beat."

"Did you arrest them right away?"

"No." The Sheriff looked at his feet. "I listened for a while—just a little while. It was a fine tune,

51

Governor, beggin' your pardon. It caught my ear as I was paddin' my beat."

Mirais nodded to the King.

The King smiled again.

"I would change the sentence," said the toad.

"*C'est bien*. Very fine. Sheriff, do you play the guitar?"

"No, Your Highness. Thought I might someday, though."

"Very well. We sentence you to learn from the court musicians how to play the guitar. Your fine is lifted." The King rapped his staff three times on the floor of the porch. "Case dismissed."

The Sheriff and the two happy farmers made to leave.

"Sheriff, one word," said the King. "Know that there are other ways to tend one's garden than with a hoe, a plow, or a spade. Sometimes a guitar will do nicely. You yourself have been lax, *très négligent*, in tending your own."

"Yes, Your Worship," said the Sheriff, looking puzzled.

As the farmers and the Sheriff were leaving, the King turned to Mirais, Mr. Trembly, and the little snake. "*Très bien*, my friend Mirais, but I fear that the Sheriff will not understand the justice of his sentence until he has mastered the guitar."

EIGHT

The Voyagers Attend the Festivities
of Harvest Day, Thereby Journeying
Still Farther Down the River

When the sun rose out of the mists above the Falls upriver from Coq d'Or in the land of Couronne, the toad, the mouse, and the snake, having slept at the King's house the night before, were already having herb tea and fruit and cereal (of which not even Mirais had ever seen so much) at the round oak table in front of the hearth. A small fire had been lit, for the morning was very chilly. There was no real chimney, but the window in the slanted rooftop served very nicely in drawing out the smoke.

Similar narrow, graceful columns of smoke rose gently from the thatch loft of every home in Coq d'Or.

The sun was climbing from behind the Falls (where the bears were already fishing in the shallows), burning away the morning mists from the River. Now the summer had passed into autumn. A chill wind tossed bright leaves in wheels and whirls into the freshly gleaned fields of the River valley. Along with the lark and the oriole, the hermit thrush was singing of autumn on that bright, clear morning.

Suddenly, a cry sounded in the village. "Your Majesty! Your Majesty! They're coming! The turtles are coming!"

The King and Queen and their guests hurried outside onto the porch. Overnight, muskrats from the two other villages of Couronne had poured into the town, and now the whole kingdom crowded the banks to see the turtles swimming downriver.

"Each year we celebrate the harvest with them," said the King to the toad, with whom he had become great friends. "The turtles help pull the barges." There were about a hundred turtles—very large ones—swimming steadily.

A feast of strawberries and blackberries and huckleberries and mulberries was laid out for them by the River. When the feast was over, the muskrats began hauling out the royal barges from the main dock. They decorated them with baskets of pink knotweed, with bergamot, and with wreaths of water fennel. The turtles, too, were decked out. There was much talk, for there had not been such a gathering since the last Harvest Day.

At noon, a company of frogs sounded a series of trumpet flourishes on snail shells. The muskrats tumbled into the water and climbed onto the barges. The musicians—crickets, and grasshoppers who played cellos and violins, frogs with their snail shells, and field mice with wooden kettledrums—were taken by boats out to the largest turtles. There, each took a seat on the back of a turtle, adjusted his music, tuned his instrument, coughed, and shuffled his feet, the way musicians will. The muskrats on the barges coughed and shuffled their feet, as audiences will.

Then the *Water Skeeter* set out from shore, all bedecked with blue gentian and orange butterfly weed. The King and Queen, the two Princes, two Marshals from the other villages, and Mirais (whose jewel shone brightly in the sun), and Mr. Trembly (who was helping the Captain with the rigging), and Glister (who was curled like a figurine on the bowsprit) were all on board.

The King raised his staff.

A trumpet sounded.

The kettledrums rolled. A cheer went up. Slowly, in stately procession, the barges, one by one, towed by the turtles, glided out softly onto the River. First, the national anthems of the muskrats and turtles were played. Then the conductor, a young muskrat in a long, black coat, white shirt, and black tie, raised his baton. The orchestra began to play the Royal Watermusic.

"It's his own composition," said the Queen, who

was dressed in the finest, cleanest, starchiest, bluest blue gown she had. She seemed very happy. "Each year a new composition is chosen for the procession and its composer conducts it." The old toad, the mouse, and the snake, to whom this had been said, nodded appreciatively.

Everyone was now seated, except for the King and the Marshals, who stood and waved to the riverfolk crowding the banks—squirrels and rabbits and badgers and chipmunks and deermice and foxes and otters—and to the riverbirds—bitterns and ducks and herons and egrets. The Captain puffed happily on his pipe and held the tiller. The whole nation of muskrats led by that of the river turtles proceeded slowly by. The kettledrums rolled thunderously. The snail shells flourished forth in piercing trills, and the fiddling crickets and grasshoppers softly bowed a melody, a melody which was as languid as the morning mist or as the flow of the River itself.

NINE

Royally Musical, Musically Royal, the Procession of Barges Comes to the Lake Isle of Innisfree

The old toad, wearing a warm sweater and a tweed jacket, sat in his deck chair watching the water drift by the bow and listening to the music. As he sat there, he noticed another procession in the water below. Leaves, gold, red, purple, and yellow, drifted slowly with the current like a flotilla of ships with sweeping, brightly colored sails. It was a sight that somewhat saddened him, the leaves filling the slow haven of the shore, and then becoming caught again in the green eddies of the River, only to break free to set sail once more on the mainstream.

"I've seen the turn of many a season, Glister,"

said the toad to the snake. Glister was now curled about a spar above Mirais's head. "And I do not have time to see many more."

"Oh, Mirais, do not talk like that. This is such a fine day and such a fine adventure." The snake was very young. One could not blame him for not wanting his day spoiled by sad talk. "Will we find Lilac soon?" asked Glister, hoping to change the conversation.

"TODAY, mate!" shouted the Captain from the stern. "Look sharp, there!" The Captain pointed over the bow with one hand as he held the tiller with the other. A broad blue expanse of calm water spread out before them. Except for a tiny, ever-so-small dot of greenish-gray far in the distance, the shining water was everywhere on the horizon.

"This, mates, is the Lake of Innisfree," the Captain said proudly, knocking his pipe's ashes on the rail— proudly, as if he himself had dug the lake's bottom. The Captain was a muskrat with an eye for good water.

The barges drifted out, one by one, onto the great lake, following the *Water Skeeter* like leaves gently pulled by the wind.

Pointing to the greenish dot on the horizon, the Captain said, "Mouse, snake, that island is where we're headed." As they crossed the lake, the musicians stopped for a rest.

Mirais spoke with the King and Queen concerning

the little girl on the island. "As far as we know," said the Queen, who was sipping a cup of herb tea, "she, poor child, is the very last human being in the forest." The Queen offered a cup of tea to Mr. Trembly. The mouse politely declined. He wasn't used to the sweetness. And this talk about the girl—what is a girl?—made him nervous. Fortunately—for the Queen was very proud of her cooking and of her herb tea, especially—Mirais and Glister took some. The Marshals were honored to have some. And the Captain was thirsty. The Queen's sons and the King knew better than to refuse. King René continued, "Until a few summers ago, Molly—that is the girl's name—did have a cousin, a third cousin, you know, rather distant, but he was a bad fellow who did some very mean things to the animals on the island." Then he said with a dark look, "The lad has not been seen since."

"Some say," said the Queen in a hushed voice, as though she were afraid, "that the White Eagle . . . who . . . lives on the mountain . . ."

"Shush, my dear," said the King. "It is better not to talk of such things." He sipped his tea as if to apologize for the command. The Queen said nothing more. Mirais understood, however, and looked thoughtfully into the water.

"Molly never seems to get older," the King said. "It would seem either that we animals age more quickly or that her good habits keep her a child."

"Pardon me, Your Majesty," said Mr. Trembly, dressed in a tweed coat, tweed cap, and tiny boots. He was so nervous about finding Lilac that he jumped up from his deck chair and started pacing in front of the King and Queen. "But why did you leave Lilac with this creature you call a girl?"

"Be calm, *mon ami*," said the King. "Molly is a mystery to us, but a nice one. She is known everywhere for her care of animals. Somehow, she knows just what to do for the malady, the broken limb, and even the broken heart. Even the snapping turtle she can make laugh. And her house is very dry and warm. Also, like your Lilac, Molly has been very lonely since her bad cousin, James, disappeared. Although he was bad in just the ways she is good, still he was the only other like her in the whole forest and lake. So, *mon ami*, do not worry for your Lilac."

It was evening before they reached the island. As they did, the King motioned to the conductor to start the music once again. Ahead, the island loomed large and green. A great many cedars and hemlocks covered the slopes. On a hillside, over which sheep were grazing, was a whitewashed stone cottage with a green, grassy roof, surrounded by an orchard. Beds of blue flowers grew beneath the windows. A red rambling rose climbed up one side.

The shore facing the procession was crowded with the island animals.

"What's . . . what's *that?*" asked Glister. One of the animals was much bigger than the others. Everyone else on the *Water Skeeter* laughed, for the animal had long, yellow hair and very blue eyes and a dress as blue as her eyes or as blue as the sky over Innisfree. She stood much taller than the other animals—and on *two* feet, sandaled with woven straw—and was clearly, even if one had never seen one before, a little girl, a pretty little girl. Embarrassed by their laughter, and to show that *he* was brave enough, Glister dropped over the side of the boat and swam to shore.

The old toad wondered, as he watched Glister making graceful S's toward the bank, his head proudly perked up, if the action would offend the King and Queen. But the King was not offended. Nor was Queen Hélène. In fact, they both were smiling.

Before the snake reached the shore, he stopped and looked up—way up for a snake—at the little girl.

"Hello," she said. "I'm Molly. What's your name?"

"Glister. Glister," said the snake.

"Are you coming ashore?"

"Yes."

"Well, let me help you." The little girl reached down into the water and gently lifted the snake. Glister wrapped himself about her wrist like a green bracelet. He looked proudly back at the *Water Skeeter* nearing the shore and the many barges being brought about behind it. Then Molly put him down on the mossy bank.

When the last blossom-bedecked turtle had pulled his barge into the shallows, King René solemnly—with his sons, the Queen, the Marshals, Mr. Trembly, and Mirais standing stiffly behind—gave the signal to stop the concert: two sharp thumps of his staff on the deck. The frogs blared one last blast on their snail shells, and the mice gave out a last, magnificent, thundering roll on their kettledrums, while the crickets and grasshoppers stilled their bows. The young muskrat conductor, flushed with the afternoon's labor, loosened his bow tie. He turned a page of music, then motioned to the grasshopper playing the first violin. The grasshopper began a very slow, rising violin solo. The conductor motioned to a mouse. A very soft, steady roll began on his drum. The drummer stopped. The grasshopper began a melody sounding like the wind easing after a spring rain, when the wind rises abruptly and then quietly falls, rises, then falls. Everyone was hushed.

"Bram!" burst the drum.

The violin played—quietly—while the water lapped the shores.

"Bram!"

The melody soared high, high as the white pines by the lake, and then low, low as the reflections of the pines on the surface of the water.

There was a pause. For a moment the conductor held his hands in the air, like birds readying for flight.

"Bram. Ba-RAM!" The watermusic was over.

A great cheer followed.

"Bravo!" shouted Mirais, clapping heartily. "Bravo!"

"Bravissimo!" shouted the two Marshals, who, after all, could not seem *less* appreciative.

The King and Queen applauded.

The young conductor bowed solemnly.

Now the island animals gathered in knots on the banks, a crowd of furry tails and whiskered faces and bright plumes and sharp beaks, and black, shiny eyes and pink, wide walleyes, and clapping paws and singing, tufted, spotted throats. All cheered, clapped, and stamped happily. And Molly did, too.

Once more the young muskrat bowed, proudly. Raising his hand, he had the orchestra rise and take a bow. With their instruments at their sides, the crickets and the grasshoppers and the frogs and the mice bowed to the King, to the island animals, to the muskrat and turtles, and to the conductor. Next the violin and drum soloists did the same. They were loudly applauded.

Finally, Captain Pelagon let down the gangplank. King René and Queen Hélène led their entourage ashore, where two rabbits gave each a bouquet of Queen Anne's lace and black-eyed Susans.

The King cleared his throat to speak. But, it seems, other matters had to be dealt with.

T E N

In Which the Writer Explains to His Reader

Do not think, dear reader, no, do not think for a minute that only Mr. Trembly was worried about Lilac. Well, perhaps Glister, it is true, got a little distracted, in all the pomp and circumstance, from what had brought them to the land of Couronne and to the Lake Isle of Innisfree. But Glister aside, as soon as they had come ashore and even before, the toad with the jewel on his forehead was looking sharply about for little Lilac, as was Mr. Trembly, whose shiny black eyes behind his spectacles searched all the heads on the shore.

And, if the bird who told me this tale told me true,

you should not think that this quest was forgotten by those in the forest who watch over everything and who cause things to be and who cause things to happen.

High in the topmost branch of the old oak that shaded the dooryard of Molly's stone cottage, a cardinal perched, watching as the *Water Skeeter* led the procession to shore.

E L E V E N

A Speech and a Discovery
Are Made

"Friends and countrymen," said the King. "We are gathered again in peace and plenty, in agreement and in good cheer. It is autumn and the end of our year's work." The white-haired King in his purple robes had climbed a platform, which the carpenter squirrels had hammered together for the occasion. As he spoke, the families of animals on the bank sat down to listen more comfortably. The muskrats of Couronne sat quietly on the anchored barges, dangling their feet in the water. The turtles floated in the clear, cool water. The old King spoke in a fine, strong voice.

"We are happy—"

"Achoo!" A sneeze sounded from among the listeners. Mr. Trembly looked at Molly. Molly blushed.

"—to celebrate—"

"Achoo!"

"Oh, dear. Excuse me," said the little girl to Mirais, sitting next to her. The King stopped to look at her.

"But my dear, was it you that sneezed?" asked the toad.

"We are happy to celebrate here together . . . ," the King gathered his words and continued, "an occasion—"

"Achoo!" Everyone turned to Molly. Molly looked down at her dress pocket. A little head poked out— "Achoo!"—and rubbed its eyes. It was a little mouse.

"Lilac!" shouted Mr. Trembly, jumping up and scurrying to her, for it indeed was she.

"She's got a cold," said Captain Pelagon.

Mirais laughed, rubbing his jewel. The King laughed, too. And so did the Queen. And so did everyone else, though they did not yet know the tale that you know.

TWELVE

Nine Bean-Rows Did She Have There
and a Hive for the Honeybee

That night, and well into the next morning, there was feasting, music, and dancing on the Lake Isle of Innisfree. And there was goat's milk and cider, yams and squashes, and all sorts of soups, and cherries and plums and peaches, and blackberry shortcake. There was plenty for everyone and even more. It was all set out on long, low tables in the yard of Molly's cottage, under the oaks. The little girl bustled back and forth from the white stone cottage, bringing hot dishes of food and chilled pitchers of milk and cider. At least three dozen squirrels, muskrats, and rabbits in bright yellow aprons hurried about, helping Molly with the food. From time to time a blue jay perched on her shoulder. "Please tell the King that the beavers from Bear Meadows have arrived," she would say, and the jay would fly off importantly to inform the King. Or she would say, "Please tell the rabbits to please hurry with the blackberries," and off flew the jay to hurry the rabbits.

Some of the creatures that lived with Molly needed her special attention even now. Scampering about was a young chipmunk that had taken sick and was now wearing a down vest and wool pants that Lilac had knit for him. Although probably old enough and well enough to take care of himself, he still pestered Molly to feed him with an eyedropper of mayapple juice and vitamins. And then there was a very ugly baby bird with a big, wobbly head. It was so young it hadn't yet opened its eyes or grown feathers. The bald bird, nest and all, had tumbled to the forest floor and been abandoned until discovered by a kindly raccoon, who had carried it to Molly. Nobody even knew what kind of bird it was. She called it Junior, and every half hour she would wipe her hands on her apron and go over to Junior in his nest on her windowsill. When she tapped the nest, Junior would wake up, raise his shaky, bald head, cheep and chirp, and open his mouth to be fed.

Then there was a wild goose, a young gander nicknamed Drifter, who only spoke to Molly and who followed her everywhere. Poor Drifter had lost his mate over the deep forest in a violent hailstorm. Now he refused to fly. Molly was trying to get him to start over.

"Drifter," she would say, "I know geese mate for life, but you can't just quit living."

But the grieving Drifter would just shake his long goose neck and say, "Oh, but she flew like a cloud, Molly, and honked so sweetly," and then waddle after Molly as she rushed to ready her kitchen.

Before the next dinner was ready, however, the younger animals competed in all kinds of contests: swimming contests, footraces, wrestling matches, boat racing. There was even a tennis match, which the last year's champion, the King's son, Claude, lost to a raccoon from the far side of the island. Some muskrats said it wasn't fair, because the raccoon had practiced every afternoon for the whole summer, while Claude had tended his field, but the King said that it was quite fair and gave the prize to the raccoon—a new cherry wood racket.

Glister entered the Swimming Contest For Speed in Open Water.

"Do you think he'll win, Mirais?" said Mr. Trembly. Lilac, in a pretty yellow dress she had made for herself (Molly had showed her how to sew), sat on her uncle's knee.

"He's got some stiff competition, mate," said the Captain, who overheard Mr. Trembly while mending his sails in the shade at the edge of the water where they were all sitting. "Mark that blacksnake. Blind me if that un's not a professional."

Lilac looked at Mirais.

"He may, my friend," said the toad. "He may just win." Mirais rubbed his forehead jewel for good luck.

Lilac clapped with excitement.

The swimmers lined up at the bank. A hundred feet out, a huge mud turtle floated. The first swimmer to reach the turtle and take a bean from his back would win. It was the major event of the day, and most of the animals had come to watch.

A water rat from the lakeshore was taking bets. "Five to one on Balboa," he called out, for the blacksnake the Captain had pointed out was the clear favorite to win.

"Five to one of what?" Mirais asked the Captain.

"They're bettin' corn ears today."

"Too bad. Too bad, indeed," said the toad, for he didn't have any to bet.

"Hey, rat! Here's a taker," shouted the Captain, dropping his sailcloth and needle. "I'll back you, mate," he whispered to Mirais. The rat, a lean-looking fellow with a brown cap pushed to one side, took the bet with a chuckle.

"THEY'RE OFF!"

The swimmers—the blacksnake, two water moccasins, a snapping turtle, and Glister—splashed from shore at the signal. A great many birds—yellow warblers, drab cowbirds, crows, and jackdaws—hovered above them to watch.

The big blacksnake kept the lead.

"C'mon, Bal-bo-a!" shouted some.

71

"C'mon, Glister!" shouted Mirais, shaking his fist in the air, and so shouted Mr. Trembly, almost falling into the water, and the Captain, who had turned in time to grab the mouse by the scruff of the neck, and Lilac, who folded her paws under her chin and danced up and down.

But Balboa kept the lead.

"Hurry, Glister!" shouted someone else from behind. It was Molly. "OH, NO! Oh, dear." She had dropped a custard pie she had let cool by the water.

The swimmers skimmed over the surface of the water. Glister, with only Balboa ahead, started moving up. The blacksnake looked angrily behind him at the sound of Glister thrashing the water. The young snake glided up to him.

"Think you're something, huh?" said the blacksnake, and he put on speed.

They were nearly to the mud turtle.

Glister moved up again. There was a great roar from the bank. Glister and the blacksnake were neck and neck.

Glister swam hard. When he heard the shouts from the bank, he put on more speed, whipping his tail in long S's. He just couldn't go any faster. But neither could Balboa, and Glister reached the mud turtle first.

"Nice race, lad," said the old turtle. "Now grab the bean." Glister reached for the bean on the turtle's knobby back, but in a wink Balboa was on the other side. With a slap of his black tail, he knocked the bean into the water.

"Foul! Foul!" screeched the birds overhead.

The two snakes dove for the bean. The other swimmers caught up and dove, too. Back on the bank, no one knew *what* to say.

"Where are they?" said Lilac.

From time to time a head bobbed up in the lake.

"They've lost the bean!" shouted the old turtle.

Meanwhile, the rat made for the spot in a row boat.

"Watch him," said the Captain.

Eventually the swimmers, except for Glister and Balboa, gave up in exhaustion.

Just as the King was about to call the race off, the two snakes came bobbing up, bodies locked and the bean in Glister's mouth.

"Gimme that!" said the blacksnake.

"Let go! Let go!" yelled the rat, trying to help the blacksnake.

"Glister wins!" said the King on the bank. The bell was rung and there was a great hullabaloo on shore, for the rat had a lot of corn to pay. Glister proudly glided into shore.

Out on the water, the rat helped the blacksnake into the boat. "A fine champ *you* turned out to be!" he said angrily.

"Aw, shut up. Let's get back."

"We can't, you dope. I can't meet those bets. They'll

skin me." The rat pointed worriedly to the crowd, which was waving at them to come in.

Mirais watched the snake and the rat arguing in the boat. He guessed the trouble and, as Glister was receiving his medal, he hopped over to the judges' platform and called up to the King in a low voice. The King leaned down. He nodded his head. The King made a special decree. "All bets have been canceled by the judges in the name of fair play. There will be no more gambling." A groan went through the crowd, but anyone could see that the games would be spoiled if the betting were continued.

The rat and the blacksnake rowed, very shamefacedly, to shore.

Late that evening, the yard was cleared for dancing. Just as the full, harvest moon rose over the lake, the musicians began to play. And everyone, it seemed, was dressed in his very finest. The King and the Queen usually began the dancing, dancing just that first dance, and for the rest of the evening they would sit under the apple trees. This time, the King insisted the evening begin with Mirais dancing with the Queen, and with Mr. Trembly dancing with his little, newly found niece.

"*Enchanté*, Your Highness," said mannerly old Mirais as he took the Queen's hand. The old toad was quick to learn the language of Couronne. The Queen curtsied and smiled. The two couples danced a waltz. After a few minutes, the other dancers joined in under the autumn moon.

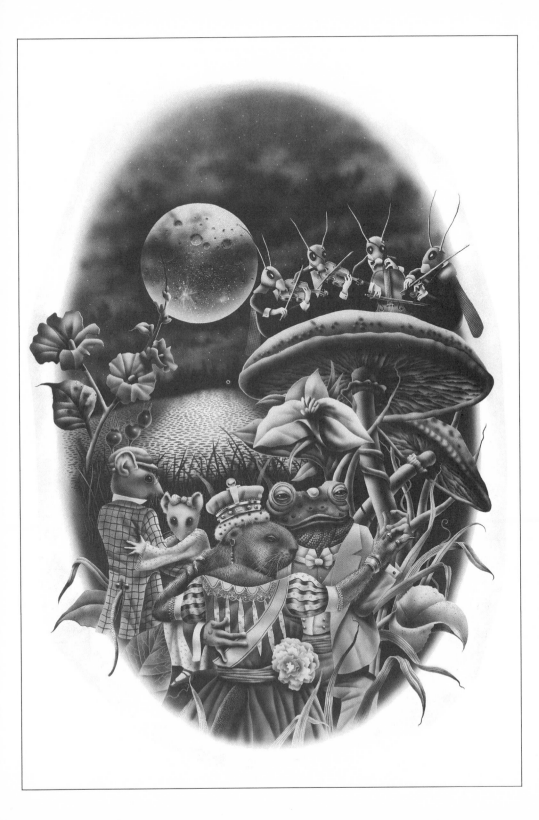

Glister, filled with his victory, curled on a branch of the tree under which the old King was seated. The King sipped some cider, watching the Queen in her freshly ironed dress dancing with the toad, who, to be honest, had, for all his gallantry, an odd little hop to his waltz step. (Well, he *was* a toad.) The King smiled, "*Cher* snake," he said, "the advantage of being a king is that one can cease to be one quite easily, and yet, *mon ami*, remain quite royal." He sipped his drink. "Dancing is an awful affair." Soon, however, the first dance was ended and, as the Queen returned with Mirais, King René put down his drink and assumed his duties once again.

"Where is Molly, Your Majesty?" asked Glister.

"Yes," said Mirais, "I haven't seen her since the music began."

The King cracked a butternut on the arm of his chair. "I do not know," he said, with a shrug of his shoulders and a twitch of his whiskered nose.

Mirais hopped off to look for her. First he searched the orchard where her sheep grazed. He hopped through the closely cropped grass. "Molly!" he called. There was no answer. Even the sheep were at the ball.

Nor was she by her little bean field, nor by her potato patch, nor by the flower garden behind her cottage. She was not at her beehives on the hillside. Mirais hopped up to the cottage. He poked his head inside the door. "Molly?" he said, softly. It was very dark inside except for a square that the moon made, shining in through the window. Inside Mirais could hear someone crying, someone crying softly to herself. The toad hopped over to the window where the young girl was sitting. Molly leaned her elbows on the sill, resting her head in her hands. The moonlight shining though the window reflected off the tears running down her cheeks. Even sad and tearful, she was a pretty girl, Mirais thought, even though he had never seen another human. With her moonlit curls and big tears, it was impossible to imagine how humans like her could fight and kill the way the legend said.

"What's wrong, child?"

Molly looked at Mirais and cried harder, hiding her face in her hands. The front of her new white dress was wet with tears.

Mirais patted her hand. "Whatever is the matter?" he said, and gave her a tiny handkerchief. He hopped up onto the windowsill.

"It's my cousin, James," she said, after she had blown her nose. "We always used to dance together at the Harvest Festival. And now I'll never see him again."

"Tell me what happened," Mirais said, cocking his head.

Molly sniffed and dabbed her eyes. "James never liked," she sobbed, "to look after things about the house. And it's true he did some mean things to animals. He tied a pot to a raccoon's tail once. I don't think he knew how mean those things were because he was very nice to me. We had so much fun.''

"Where did he go?'' asked Mirais.

"Nowhere at all.'' She began to cry again.

"Where is he then?'' said the toad.

"One day when we were walking on the hill he teased an owl that couldn't see its way home in the daylight. The owl was very old and very angry. He warned James to watch out. But James just laughed. I warned him, too. He laughed again and his hair turned green and leafy. He tried to grab the owl, but he couldn't move his feet, for his toes had grown very long and twisted and they dug into the ground. I pleaded with the owl to stop, but before I could finish, the owl turned into a crow and flew away. James's legs then turned to wood and grew together. Soon he was all green and woody. And there he was, a willow tree, weeping by the brook near the end of the orchard.''

"Hmm,''said Mirais, remembering what the Queen had said of the White Eagle. "Hmm,'' he said, scratching his forehead.

"Oh, Mirais, how would you feel? He was the only one like me in the whole world and now he's just a tree by the water!''

"Hmm,'' said the wise old toad, and he patted her hand.

THIRTEEN

Discussions on a Shady Bank

"Es-tu sûr, mon ami?" said the King. "Mirais, my friend, are you sure you should do this?" It was two days later. Down by the lake's edge, under an overcast sky, the muskrats were readying their barges for the return to Couronne. Mirais and the King sat across from each other on two logs by the water. The old King sat with his furry cheek against his staff, which he held in his right hand. Mirais sat beneath a beech tree, whittling a stick. The Captain leaned against the tree and smoked his pipe, his hands shoved deep into the pockets of his baggy gray trousers. Nearby sat Mr. Trembly, intent, it seemed, upon splitting a beech

leaf into strips. Next to him Glister was curled in the hollow of a broken branch like a dark ring left by rainwater. Nobody said anything, not even Mirais, for a long time.

"It is worth a try, Your Majesty. How far is the sea, Captain?" said the toad. "How far?"

"A week of walking, mate. Less than two days by boat."

"Which way is it?" asked Mr. Trembly, tossing away the shredded beech leaf.

"Due west. The River opens out again on the far side of the lake and runs a bit, slows down some, and runs into her." The Captain puffed steadily on his pipe.

"Will you go with us, Captain Pelagon?" said Glister hopefully.

The Captain looked at the King, for, after all, he was first obligated to pilot the King, the Queen, their sons, and the two Marshals back to Couronne.

"Of course he will," said the King. "That is, *if* you are going, Mirais."

Mirais looked at the young snake and at the mouse and at the muskrat captain.

"Mouse," said the King, "have you come so far and for so long with so many dangers in search of Lilac that you should risk never seeing her again?"

Mr. Trembly looked uncomfortably toward Molly's cottage high on the hill. Lilac was flying a kite in the yard. Mr. Trembly looked down at his feet and did not answer.

"And did you not promise to return Glister safely to his parents, Mirais?"

Mirais shook his head, but kept on whittling. Then he stopped. "My lord," he said, brushing the front of the new woolen sweater the girl had made for him, "this little girl has done us a great service in caring for Lilac. She has been good to us all. If she is unhappy because of her cousin, then we must make her happy once more. I am sure, Your Majesty, that if Lilac were never to see us again she would be well cared for in Innisfree."

"But what of the White Eagle?"

"A ruler of the air such as he," said the toad, "would not, by my jewel, deserve to rule if he harmed such as we."

King René stood up straight. He looked at the toad on the log, at the Captain leaning against the tree, and at Mr. Trembly and Glister sitting on the branch. He smiled broadly as he spread his arms wide, holding his staff a little raised. "You are certain of the rightness of your mission, *mes amis*, and your certainty is right." He thumped the butt of his staff in the dust. "Go and find the White Eagle who rules the air and all that moves in it, who rules the forest and the meadow, the lake and the shore, to whom no one has ever spoken, for, by Saint Bertilak, if a boy can become a willow, surely a willow can be changed into a boy!"

FOURTEEN

Farewells

That afternoon, under a cloudy sky, the three adven-
turers made ready to leave with Captain Pelagon.
Mr. Trembly, bustling about the deck of the *Water
Skeeter*, gathered together the provisions for the trip.
Little Lilac was by his side, very curious about the
mysterious journey. There was water, and bread, and
cereal to be fetched on board, and blankets, for the
nights were now very cold. When Molly brought a
basketful of cheese and apples down from her cottage
on the hill, she, too, asked the mouse why it was they
had to make this trip downriver.

"Oh . . . well . . . ah . . . Captain Pelagon just

wants to show us the sea," he said, for Mirais had warned him to say nothing in case their mission was a failure.

"Oh," said Molly, folding napkins into the basket.

"You'll be back soon, Uncle Trembly, won't you?" said little Lilac, looking up, a bit tearfully, to the mouse as he took the basket from Molly.

"Of course," he said.

"And then we'll go back to the Pond?"

"And never leave," he said, whisking off his tweed cap and giving Lilac a hug.

Just then Glister came swimming to shore from the dock where the muskrats were making ready to return to Couronne. "Molly, Lilac, come on! Mr. Trembly, hurry! The King is ready to leave." The snake dropped down into the water, turned about, flicked his long green tail, and swam back to the dock.

When Molly ran to the dock (with Mr. Trembly and Lilac tucked in a sweater pocket), muskrats had already boarded the barges. The animals from the island were waiting to wave good-bye, good-bye until the next year. A little rain began to patter the surface of the lake, which was dark as the color of the clouds. Standing on the dock next to the King, Queen Hélène looked anxiously at her newly pressed dress. She opened an umbrella and held it over the King's head as they prepared to say farewell. *"Il pleut,"* she said. *"Mes amis,"* said the King, "good luck!"

Mirais, the Captain, the mouse, and the snake

bowed low. The Queen, God bless her, began to sniffle. A tear rolled down her cheek and splattered on her dress. "Be careful," she said. The King frowned. No one wanted Lilac or Molly to be frightened.

The Queen smiled bravely. She would have kissed the little girl good-bye, but thought it awkward to ask to be lifted up.

"Good-bye, Your Majesty," said Molly, who, poor child, was sniffling, too. She curtsied, holding her little blue dress by the hem with the fingers of both hands.

"Be good, Lilac," said the Queen, "and *you*, too, Glister, Mirais."

Mirais bowed and kissed her paw, gallant fellow that he was. Then he made a sharp nod of his head to Mr. Trembly. The mouse quietly retreated to the shore.

"Return to Couronne, my friends," said the King, and he gave Mirais a cedar cane, all twisted and dark with age. "Take this. Remember *La Cheminée du Roi René*. Remember never to neglect your garden."

"And these," said the Queen, holding in both her arms four folded black capes and four woolen black caps. "They'll keep you warm, nights."

Mr. Trembly returned carrying a large bouquet of white, sweet-smelling roses. He gave them to the Queen, who gasped with pleasure. The King smiled. "*Allons*," he said, "it is time to depart." As he boarded a barge, he signaled the musicians. The conductor looked uncertainly at the sky, turned a page of music, and raised his baton. The orchestra began to play. The animals on shore cheered. The muskrats cheered. The turtles pulled the barges out into the lake, the King's barge, of course, went first. Herons and ducks, large flappers, cried above, circling and swooping low. The muskrats waved to their friends on shore. The music played. Mirais looked down to examine his cane. There was a gold cock on the end of the cane, the bird of Coq d'Or. There was a real red feather stuck to its tail. A cardinal's tail feather, it was. "By my jewel," said the toad to himself. When he looked up to shout bon voyage, the barges were already too far away for the toad to be heard. Soon the barges were just dots on the horizon, and only strains of music could still be heard drifting in with the wind. Soon they were out of sight.

A few minutes later, when the squirrels, and the otters, the chipmunks, the rabbits, and the ground-hogs and the field mice, and the beavers and the foxes and the raccoons and the badgers and the possums and the owls and the bitterns and the ducks and the flycatchers and the egrets and the blackbirds, and all the rest of the animals and birds who lived on the island, went home, Molly, brown-skinned and blue-eyed, and Lilac, sitting on the little girl's shoulder, were left alone on the dock as the *Water Skeeter* was being made ready to sail. The Captain rang the bell, then he took out a long silver bo'sun's pipe and piped his crew on board. Its high and steady, reedy trill cut the silence of the deserted, lake-lapped shore. "Trim the sails, snake! Up anchor, mouse! Hoist flag, toad!" Everyone hopped to. "Don't you worry now," he shouted to Lilac and Molly. "Don't you worry now, my pretties. We'll sail in afore the eighth bell on the ninth day of the tenth month, afore Orion finds Aldebaran, afore the Dog Star wags his tail."

Jumping up on Molly's shoulder, Lilac waved.

"Be good, Lilac!"

"I will, Uncle."

"Good luck, Mirais."

"Thank you, child. Take care."

Soon, too, the *Water Skeeter* was out of sight. Lilac scampered down Molly's shoulder and into her dress pocket. As Molly climbed the hill, all thick now with ragweed, clover, and Queen Anne's lace, the only sounds were those of the wind hushing through the tall hemlocks and the sheep's bells lazily dangling-clanging under their throats as the animals slowly grazed about the orchard by the grass-roofed, white-washed stone cottage.

FIFTEEN

Why They Went to the Sea
and What They Found There

The Captain sat in the stern. The snake was by the prow. And the toad was watching the wind as it battered the sails. The mouse, coiling rope, asked some pertinent questions. "Mirais," he said, "why is it we're going to the sea, and . . . Mirais, what *is* the sea?"

"Yes," said Glister, "is the White Eagle there?"

Mirais rubbed his jewel, thought a moment, and began,

> "*Larger waves than on any lake*
> *Crash by the ocean's shore.*
> *On sandy bars the water breaks*
> *Saltier by much more*

Than any you've swum before, snake,
Than any you've swum before.

There's seabirds by the water's edge:
Pelicans, gulls, and more,
Which dibble and dabble and fish the sedge
That grows by the seashelled shore.
More birds than you've seen before, mouse,
More birds than you've seen before.

White Eagle is no ocean bird,
Though he rules the wave-swept shore.
Where he dwells none has heard
If it's cliff or green valley floor.
For no one's been there before, friends,
For no one's been there before.''

"Then why are we going to the sea?'' asked Glister.

"To see someone who can tell us how to find the White Eagle.''

"But you said no one knew.''

"This one can find out, snake. Just this one. No one else.''

"Who?''

Mirais shot a glance at Captain Pelagon. "Robertus Magnus, the blind mole, the magician who lives by the sea.''

"Oh,'' said Glister.

"Oh,'' said Mr. Trembly.

"*Magus Sciens*, Doctor Polymathus, he is, my friends. I met him once a long time ago, in the deep woods. He was looking for bones."

"Bones!" said Glister, turning about the deck rail like a grapevine on a trellis.

"To make potions with."

"Oh," said Glister, thinking it better not to ask what potions were.

"He's not a bad fellow—unless you cross him."

The *Water Skeeter* crossed the lake under full sail. That evening they dropped anchor near a marshiest, boggiest, swampiest shore. Herons and egrets and bitterns were all about. The trees hung heavy with thick draperies of moss. The branches seemed slimy. Roots twisted as if alive. The moon was up, and owls were hunting in its silver light. Low-hanging branches dragged the water. Glister was scared. A mist crept upriver, swirling about the bow. Night came. Strange sounds slapped the surface of the water. Eerie hootings hung in the air like frosty breath in winter.

The Captain lit the firefly lamps. Before they went to bed, they ate some baked apples and drank some goat's milk.

"Mates, we'll post watch tonight. Two hours apiece."

All that night one of them paced the deck, darkly garbed in a cloak and cap. All night each in his turn paced the deck, watching, listening, keeping a sharp ear, guarding as the mist swirled about and flooded the deck—mist, blind as a mole.

With the light of morning, they set sail. They sailed into the afternoon until the River, which had been very swift and broad, broke into many sandy and snaky byways, channels, and cross-passages. The Captain stopped the boat. He looked at a chart. First he held it one way. He scratched his head. Then he turned it upside down, or for all you know or I know (or for all he knew) right side up, perhaps. The Captain knocked some ashes from his pipe. He slapped his cap against the rail.

"Which way, Captain?" said Mr. Trembly.

"Blind me if I know, mate." The Captain ran his finger across the corner of the map where it was dotted with islands and choked with fishnets of channel markings. "We're around here somewhere," he said. All four bent over the map. The sun flooded the deck with hazy, autumn glow.

"Now, where do ye be, Cap'n?" rasped a voice overhead. They looked up. A crow with one true leg and one wooden leg perched on the mainspar.

"Don't know, mate," said the Captain.

"Might ye be lookin' for ol' Blind Bob the Mole?"

"Yes," said Glister. "How did you know?"

"Squawk-squawk-squaw-ah-ah-awk," laughed the crow in a very nasty way. Glister looked at Mirais. "If ye want to find him, follow me," said the crow abruptly, and he flapped off down a narrow waterway.

"Why not, mates?" said the Captain. They put off after him, a muggy breeze filling their sail. The crow

91

flapped on just ahead of the bow. For an hour or more, he continued to lead them down narrow and dark channel ways, in many places so narrow that the trees from both banks entirely joined overhead to block out the sun. Little golden-finned fishes skirted beneath their prow. The rigging became snarled with broken-off willow switches and Spanish moss.

"He's going to lead us aground!" Mr. Trembly shouted to the toad. "Look how shallow the water is." He pointed to the weedy bottom.

Just then they cleared a bend and arrived at an ancient wharf. The rotted plankings and pilings were withered and gray, green and mossy. Long splits and cracks seamed the slippery grain.

The crow flew off over the trees without a word.

"Captain!" shouted Mirais.

"Never ye mind," said the Captain. "Look here." He pointed to a spot on his map. The old wharf was marked on it. So was a trail. The Captain pointed to a trail winding into the woods. "There. There's our way, lads."

It was now late afternoon. Mr. Trembly got the packs out while the others tended to the *Water Skeeter*, mooring her to the old wharf. "I don't feel right leavin' her here," said the Captain, pointing to the wharf. "Why, mark those pilings." Mirais and the Captain walked over the creaky boards. "They're rotted. Why, they're no stronger than milkweed stalks." Captain Pelagon kicked at one. "A storm could take the whole dang-blasted wharf away—and the *Skeeter*." He shoved his hands into his pockets and shook his head.

"Might someone harm her?" asked Mr. Trembly.

"Take a pretty ornery critter to do that, it would."

"Just the same," said the snake, who called back to the wharf from the end of the trail where he had already been poking about, "why not put a sign up or something, to warn folks off?"

"Indeed," said Mirais, "it isn't a bad idea."

The Captain thought it was a good idea too, and as the toad, the mouse, and the snake waited on the wharf, he climbed the rail and went aboard the *Water Skeeter* to fashion a sign.

The three sat on the old wharf and looked about. It was a quiet, sleepy place. The water was green with scum and eelgrass. Lily pads clustered across the water's surface. White-spired bugbanes and purple pickerelweeds crowded to the water's edge and filled the marshy meadow. Occasionally a bass or a sunfish would jump after a dragonfly, for there were many skimming over the lily pads. And occasionally a bird— perhaps a hungry shrike or a frightened heron—would shatter the silence with a nerve-splitting shriek.

"Will we need *two* packs, Mirais?" asked Mr. Trembly.

"No, let's fill one with a little cheese and a few apples and some blankets. We'll take turns carrying it."

The Captain returned to the deck with an old square

of sailcloth rolled under his arm. "This'll take care of her," he called down. As he spoke, he let the banner roll out, showing the warning.

"Oh!" said Glister, darting back quickly. Mirais and Mr. Trembly gulped. It was a most terrifying banner: a bright red and very evil eye above two crossed bones.

With a dark laugh that did not become him, the old Captain hung it over the bow rail, facing the wharf. "I warrant this'll keep 'em off my deck," he said as he climbed down. But standing on the wharf, he gave a shudder as he examined his handiwork. "Aye," he said, "maybe it do be a mite too strong, snake."

"Let it be. Let it be," said Mirais.

"It serves its purpose," said the mouse as he shouldered his pack, stuck his head into the tumpline, and leaned his forehead into it, adjusting his glasses and testing the weight of the pack. The homebody mouse had become quite a hiker. Meanwhile, the Captain drew out his map to find his bearings. Then he led the questers into the dark, green, wet, and very silent forest. Mirais, carrying his gold, cock-studded cane, followed the Captain. Mr. Trembly followed him, pack on his back, the red feather left him by the cardinal at the Pond tied on a string about his furry neck. Young Glister, the very green of the water, darted, now fore, now aft, rapidly this way and that across puddles and pools, across lily pads and over roots.

"Home's fine enough, Mirais," said Glister, "but I don't ever want to go back. Nothing happens at the Pond. Why, the Pond's just a puddle compared to Innisfree."

"Humph!" said Mr. Trembly. What unkind things, he thought, to have to hear about his pond. Why, didn't a new rat move in just last year? And who cared for water, anyway? "Well, you may just *not* get a *chance* to see the Pond again," he said angrily.

Glister stopped. "Why do you say that?" He looked very troubled. Glister remembered his uncles, Alcor and Mizar, both braver, bigger snakes than he.

"Oh, I was just joking, snake," said the mouse, for immediately he regretted having frightened Glister.

"Yes, he was joking," said Mirais. "I see no reason," he said with a grin of his toothless jaws,

> *"I see no reason why*
> *For either you or I*
> *Or the mouse or the Captain*
> *To fear what may happen,*
> *For the Eagle won't harm us,*
> *Nor shall the mole charm us.*

"Come," he said, "it's getting late." But Glister stood still. "Come, come-come-come," Mirais said, twirling his cane, and smiling. The Captain laughed. Finally Glister budged from his lily pad and they got under way again, wandering through the tangled, twisting paths of the swamp until evening. Often the Captain consulted his map, and, often, it was the mere look of the trails or the way of the wind that decided their route.

"We could wander here all night, Mirais," said Mr. Trembly.

"Put by your troubles now, mate," said the Captain, who had stopped and taken a deep breath through his nose. "I can smell the sea over there." He pointed to the west, from where the wind was blowing and where the sun was falling into the treetops, setting the moss curtains afire with its last, red light.

Yet when they came out of the swampy forest and into a clearing it was not the sea they saw, but a far less welcome sight.

"What, what in the world is it?" said Mr. Trembly. All stood dead in their tracks.

"Jumpin' jackfish!" said the Captain. His mouth hung open. "Gar my hide!"

"By my jewel," said Mirais. They looked out upon a vast field of bones, of tattered scraps of clothing hanging about the bones, skeletons, large orange heaps of rusting metal, and rusting shells like the one which made the mouse's house back on Duck Hill. Swallows and nighthawks darted low, swooped low over the field. "By my jewel, an awful battle was fought here. And those were men."

"Look!" said Glister. The crow with the wooden leg perched atop a rusting heap of metal. "Well come," he said. "Squawk. Caa-Caah. What's the trouble? Where have you been? Catching blueflies? Squaw-aw-awK! Blind Bob's been waitin' on ye." The crow flapped away over the bone field.

Mirais looked at Mr. Trembly.

Mr. Trembly looked at the Captain.

The Captain looked at Mr. Trembly.

Glister looked at them all.

Without a word, they trekked across the field, following the crow, careful to avoid the bones and the scraps of sharp, twisted metal. When they had crossed, they looked back with a shudder. What animals, they thought, would spoil themselves so violently, so hopelessly, and with such awful carnage and waste? Mirais took the red feather in his hand that King René had affixed to the cane cock's tail. He held the feather above his head. The ocean breeze caught it. The red feather fluttered. The Captain took off his cap and looked at his feet. Mirais let the feather go. It sailed across the ancient battlefield with the wind, landing in the middle.

"Come," said Mirais, turning to take the pack from the mouse. He patted the snake on the head. "Come, let's find Robertus Magnus." The wise old toad led the way down the craggy, sheer, seaside cliff.

S I X T E E N

Strange Happenings

Gulls flew just above their heads, fluttering their wing tips not a rat's whisker away, keening like wives who have lost their husbands, for indeed, some say gulls are the souls of sailors' wives, sailors who have drowned at sea. "Where . . . WHERE'S THE HOME . . . OF THE . . . MAGICIAN?" shouted the Captain to them, but either they did not hear or they were frightened, for at that, the gulls veered far off over the water.

"It's around here somewhere. The old mole told me he lived in a cliff cave," said Mirais, testing the way with his cane.

"Do way! Do WAY! Do WAY! Wiel-a-way and Well-a-day! Where are they, you simple-minded, black, bedeviled crow?"

The four stopped. They listened. Just over their heads, they saw an iron lantern bolted to a rock. Beside that was a dark entrance from which the voice, shrill and angry, had come.

"But, Bob, I told them the way!" answered a raspy plea.

"That's the crow," whispered the mouse to the toad.

"Bob! Bob, is it? *Robertus Magnus*, you insolent black'rd. O-o-oh, but I have means to teach your black heart a thing or two and keep you silent, as well!"

"Cawk! Cawk! Cawk!" cried the crow.

"What's he doing to him?" Glister whispered to the Captain. Then there was a flash of light, and a puff of smoke belched from the dark entrance. Then it was quiet. The four stood still, not knowing what to do. As they stood there, organ music, slow and somber, poured from the cave.

"I'll go up," said Mirais. "He knows me." The old toad returned the pack to Mr. Trembly. He rubbed the jewel on his forehead, then climbed up to the entrance. The others watched him anxiously.

"Oh, dear," said the mouse.

"Hush," said the Captain. The organ continued to play. When Mirais reached the ledge where the lantern was hanging, he noticed a sign cut in the stone beneath the lantern.

A snake swallowing its tail formed a circle in which was a triangle, and inside of the triangle was the name *Robertus Magnus*.

There was a great deal of chalk dust on the ledge floor. From out of the cave came an acrid smell of sulfur. The music continued. Mirais did not wish to interrupt. Although it was too dark inside to see well, he noticed in a corner the old mole at the organ. The mole scrambled, pulling the stops, shutting them, pumping the worn, wooden pedals with his small feet, scampering over the keyboard of the oversized instrument. He looked very much like a huge spider, for the mole moved feverishly, yet deftly, darkly, and with utter intent. Despite the oddity of the mole, the music soared out of the rock's heart chambers with great grace and countermelody. The mole, at last, stopped. He wiped his forehead. Mirais looked about for the crow, but he was nowhere to be seen.

"O *Magus Sciens*," said the toad. "I beg your pardon, but you will remember our meeting in the wood?"

The mole turned sharply about. "Mirais, I've been expecting you. Where are your friends, the mouse, the snake, and old Captain Pelagon?" Hesitantly, Mirais pointed outside. "Bring them in," said the mole. Mirais wondered how the mole knew of their coming. He summoned the others.

Rather gravely, they all shook hands.

"How did you know of our coming?" asked the toad boldly.

The mole smiled a not very winning or friendly smile. He had very few teeth. "Oh, Mirais . . . heh . . . heh . . . I have ways. How was I finding bones that day, blind as I was, blind as I am? Come, come sit down. Mr. Trembly, my lad, bring that pot over and we'll have some tea."

Mr. Trembly went over to a dark corner of the cave where some pots were hissing on a very black, dirty stove. He lifted the lid of a pot and looked in. "Oh! Ugh!" he cried, slamming down the lid.

"Not that pot, you fool!" screamed the mole, crashing his fist on the table.

"What did you see?" cried Glister, coiling himself about a clear glass ball on the table.

"A dead bat . . . with . . . a fish's face," said the mouse shakily. The mole pushed him aside and fetched the right teapot, but no one wanted any tea.

"Well, well, well-a-day," said the mole with an ugly laugh, "so you don't like my tea, well, well."

As their eyes grew accustomed to the dark, somewhat aided by a smelly oil lamp on the table, the four noticed many strange things about the cave, for there were all manner of charts and maps of the stars hung on the walls. There was a heavy black cauldron turned upside down in one corner, very big it was, about the size of the old mud turtle who held the bean in the water at Innisfree. There was a long telescope, which pointed at the evening sky through a hole in the wall. There were playing cards on the table before them, very strangely pictured. One showed a tower being struck by lightning as two human beings were cast from its height. *The Tower* it read underneath. Another showed two dogs barking at the moon by a shore. A scorpion crawled from the sea behind them. *The Moon* it read underneath. On top of the organ was a little statue of a crow. Really, it wasn't a *little* statue at all. It was the same size as a live crow. "Why, that looks just like the crow who showed us the way," said Glister, for indeed the statue had one wooden leg.

Mirais coughed loudly.

"Hee-hee," said the mole, putting his thumb to the side of his cheek. "Why, that's Nubian all right. Right you are, my little green fellow."

"But—" said Glister.

"Oh now, he'll be all right," the mole laughed. "Praise Baal, he'll be as quiet as stone. Hee. Hee."

"See here, mate," said the Captain, getting up angrily. "That bird was no prize, but—"

"I'm sure Robertus will have him back," said

Mirais, smiling forcedly. The Captain seemed about to grab the mole.

"What? Why . . . of . . . oh, yes, of course," said the mole, seeing the toad's intent. "Yes, yes. Just wanted to teach him a little lesson. He was to have brought you three hours ago."

"Humph!" said the Captain, sitting down slowly. But even before he was seated, the crow was alive again. It flapped its wings and picked its breast feathers.

"Fetch the chalk, you black-hearted ingrate, or I'll clip your wings for good—for bad, that is." The mole liked his own joke. Without a word, the crow flew off the organ and out into the air. "Mirais," said the mole, paying no attention to their stares outside, "this card is your Significator. It is the King of Cups. You are a quester, my aged friend. The Ace of Swords, as you see, Covers you. You have authority." The mole continued to turn the cards. "Authority. So do not worry if the High Priestess has brought the mysterious into Your House," he said turning down still another card and laughing at his private joke.

"Shall we meet the White Eagle?" asked the toad. All were now seated at the table. They watched the mole, who never opened his eyes. The mole laughed a shrill little laugh. He turned a card, but kept his head straight up. Yet he called its name rightly. "The Hierophant is what Lies Ahead," the mole said. He turned another. "The Emperor is What Will Be. Yes, of course, you shall meet the White Eagle. At dawn, you'll meet him. And were it not for you, my friends, and your good mission, I, sorcerer that I am, would never have met him, for all my magic circles cannot snare him unless there's good in them, unless he chooses to come. You, unlikely folk from a nobody pond, will do me a great service and I, Robertus Magnus, shall return the service at the very moment daylight breaks over the waves." The mole laughed darkly to himself. He got up from the table and walked to a corner, where he laid himself down on a cot. Without even a goodnight, he went to sleep.

The toad coughed. The four looked at one another. "I'll get the milk and the apples," said the mouse, nervously going to the ledge.

"And the cheese and the blankets," said the snake, hurrying after him.

"Better get our cloaks and caps," said Mirais to the mouse. The Captain began to light a fire. Mirais looked about. "We'll sleep here tonight," he said.

SEVENTEEN

Conjurations

On the beach at dawn, the pipers waded in the chill, shallow pools, stabbing for starfish with their scissor bills. Gulls gabbled about, but at a safe distance, as the toad, the mouse, the snake and the muskrat captain quietly stood by the mole in their warm black capes. The mole made a last notation of the stars in a large, heavy black book. "It is time," said the mole. He, too, was dressed in a black cape, a cape cut in four pieces, at the front and back, and at the sides. His head was bare. The cold wind from the ocean nipped his gray scalp. Mornings, evenings, and nights were very cold, for winter was close coming. The crow hobbled obediently at the mole's side.

Sleepy and a bit achy in his back from the cave's damp, Mr. Trembly wondered if he ought to help, somehow, with the preparations. "No! No, be off!" said the mole at the mouse's offer. "Go and stand over there with your friends. One slight error, one unknowing word, one word left out, could bungle the whole conjuration. By Saleos, be off, I say. This is no songbird we're summoning, but the White Eagle. Four bites from that beak of his and we'd all be done for. Be off."

Mr. Trembly retreated to his friends as the crow returned with a black, dusty bag of charcoal dust in his bill. "Nice lad, Nubian. Now fetch the Knife of the Art from my table." Silently, the crow flew back to the cave in the cliff. "Mouse . . . there is one thing. Fetch me the rope—you and the snake there, go fetch it—that lies wrapped in cloth by the telescope." The mouse and the snake took off together, leaving in the sand a broken, curvy track next to a little tail-and-paw printed one. Mirais and the Captain were left alone with the mole.

"I don't like it, mate. How do we know what that one's up to?" The Captain sat down abruptly on a weathered log half buried in the white sand.

Mirais turned over in his hands a deep blue shell. He sat by the Captain on the smooth, deep-grained log. "Captain," he said, "we've got no choice. Indeed, as I see it, we've got no choice at all."

"What be all that jibber-jibber and jangelering?

Blind my eyes, mate, he could do to us what he did to the crow."

"No, he won't, Captain. At worst, he will just fail in bringing the White Eagle. S-ssh!" said the toad, throwing the shell down. "He's coming over."

"Well, what do we have here? A little meeting of the minds?" The mole, his four-sectioned cloak waving in the sea wind, stalked over. "Well-a-day. Captain," said the mole, "Captain—bah!" The mole kicked a ball of seaweed that the cold, autumn wind had carried to his feet. He turned on his heel and walked back to where he had cleared and smoothed an area free of stones, driftwood, and crackled seashells.

"Let's sit down," said Mirais to the Captain. The Captain stood beside him, puffing angrily on his pipe, staring at the mole. Mirais turned his collar up against the wind. "Here come the others." The snake and the mouse returned with the rope.

The mole moved quickly at his work. He took the silver knife the crow had fetched and plunged it deep in the white, freshly smoothed sand. ("Is he *really* blind?" asked the snake. "I don't know," answered the toad, "he appears to have better sight than you or I.") Robertus Magnus next tied the rope to the knife. The free end of the rope—just nine feet from the knife—he gave to the crow. The crow put it in his bill. "Be a good lad and walk about, Nubian." The crow began walking—rather, limping—pulling his wooden leg stiffly behind him. When the crow had made a full turn about the knife, the tip of his wooden leg had made a perfect circle in the sand. "Hee-hee-hee," laughed the mole shrilly. "Why, he's better than a compass." Mirais, Glister, Mr. Trembly, and the Captain stood silently together and watched. "I ought to wring his neck," mumbled the Captain as he chewed his pipestem in anger.

"Here ye be," said the crow, giving Robertus Magnus the rope. "By your leave, I'll be going home." The mole, who had no further use for the crow, paid no attention to him. The crow flew off over the sand toward the cliff.

The mole began filling the circular furrow with charcoal dust, shaking it, a little at a time, from the mouth of the bag. When he finished, he took some colored pieces of wood from another bag and made a fire. "Mind it doesn't go out," he ordered Glister, who was the coldest of the four, and who, indeed, became sluggish and sleepy with the cold. "Take out a chip now and then from the pack. And, mind, touch nothing else inside. It's not for heat that I lit this fire, but it will, nevertheless, keep you comfortable." The fire glowed green and amber and blue. It sent sweet-smelling drifts of smoke over the black edge of the circle.

When the sun began to appear over the dune in the East, the mole made a smaller circle about five feet from the first in the direction of the cliffs. He made this smaller circle with the twigs of an elder tree on which the sun never shone. *"E-L,"* he said in a clear voice, as he wrote the letters with his fingers. The mole stared at his handiwork. "It is a fearful name," he said to the mouse and the toad and the old Captain. Slowly he wiped his hands with a red cloth.

In the direction of the sea, in a perfect line with the sun, with the Circle of El, and with the Great Circle, he made another small one. He made it with ivory sticks carved from the tusks of a walrus. *"A-G-L-A,"* he said as he spelled out the letters in the sand with his fingers. "Agla is a powerful name," he said, and he wiped his fingers with a sea-green cloth.

He made a third circle, due south, it was. He made it with a pair of horns, which a deer had dropped in midsummer when the sun was high. *YAH* was the name he wrote with his hand and which he spoke out loud. He dusted some sand from his hands with a blue cloth. "Much comes from this," he said, pointing to the Circle of Yah. The wind whipped his four-sectioned cloak.

The old mole—Dr. Polymathus, he was sometimes called—shouted to Mirais, who was poking the sand with the cane given to him by the goodwilled King of Couronne. "Give me your stick," he said, "for only with it can I complete this fearful circle to the North, this Circle, which shall contain the most potent of names save one."

"No," said Mirais, looking at the mole's outstretched hand. "First, by my jewel, I'll have your

word—your word, by that most powerful name—
that you'll use this cane for no evil end."

"Give it here!" screamed the mole in a shrill voice.

"No, no, my friend. First, swear."

"You do not trust me," screamed the mole. He
kicked the sand at his feet. "Here!" He shoved his
hand out for the cane.

"No," said Mirais. "Swear."

The mole shook with rage. He bit his finger. "I
swear," he said at last. "I, Robertus Magnus," he
continued, for well he knew how to make a pact, "do
swear by Adonay to use this wood for no evil end."
He gritted his teeth. "Now give it here," he grumbled.
The toad gave him the cane with the golden cock on
top.

To the North, the mole made the Circle of Adonay.
He made it with Mirais's cane. He wrote the name in
the sand with his fingers. Then he wiped his hands
with a white cloth. He put the elder branches, the
walrus tusks, and the deer's antlers in his sack, but
he kept the cane with the golden cock handle. With
it he made a square, joining the Circle of El with the
Circle of Yah and the Circle of Yah with the Circle of
Agla and the Circle of Agla with the Circle of Adonay.
It was a double-sided square. In the center of each of
its four sides he wrote a single word. He returned the
cane to Mirais. "This is the most powerful of numbers," said the mole as he spelled the word in the
sand: *T-E-T-R-A-G-R-A-M-M-A-T-O-N*. The mole
looked about him and at the sun, which had risen

higher over the cliffs in the East. "Hand me that purple sack," he said to Mr. Trembly. The mole pointed to a small, dusty sack of chalk dust. The mouse brought the sack. "Do not," warned the mole, "step over the edge of any of these sacred perimeters. Not yet. Here . . . hand me that." The mouse leaned fearfully over the line named Tetragammaton, handing the sack to the mole. Then he returned to the fire where Glister and Mirais and Captain Pelagon were standing.

"I don't like it," muttered the Captain.

Robertus Magnus emptied the purple chalk into the furrows of the four circles and the square he had just finished. The lines and letters stood out boldly against the white sand. "I don't like it," repeated the Captain as they walked over to see. So far the magical borders looked like this:

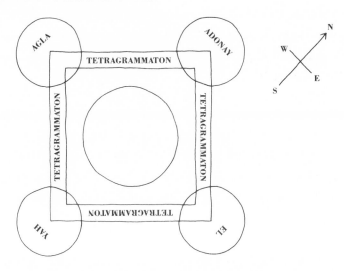

"Look!" cried Mr. Trembly, pointing to the dunes

113

farther off. In wheeling circles, shadows broke on the beach and across the dunes.

"But there's not a bird or beast over there," said Glister. "Who is making them?" They all looked at the mole.

"Enter these sanctified precincts. Let the fire smoke." The mole made a break in the line called Tetragrammaton. Glister quickly skirted in. Mirais followed. Then the Captain. Then the mouse. The magician sealed the square once more. The shadows came from the North and from the South, and from the East and the West. One darkened the face of the cliff. One passed like a black cloud from the sea to the shore. One came down from up the beach. One came up from down the beach. The wind picked up quickly and began to howl, tumbling green, salty balls of seaweed across the beach and raising a cloud of flying sand. The sand pelted the five standing in the square. The wind whipped their clothes. They crouched low with their backs to it.

"Do something!" cried the snake, who was almost covered with sand.

The mole smiled. He raised his arms high above his head. "AGLON. TETRAGRAM. VAYCHEON!" he shouted into the wind. "May all devils flee who would harm this Circle!" The winds quieted. Yet, on that cloudless day, a shadow lurked in each of the circles at the ends of the square. The mole laughed at the wriggling snake nearly buried in the sand. "When

I complete the Inner Circle, be ready to step inside." The mole entered the circle. He placed a black, four-cornered hat on his head. Inside the circle he wrote the word *VORAX*. "Enter," he commanded. The snake and the mouse and the toad and the muskrat Captain rushed into the Great Circle. The mole filled the letters of the word with purple chalk. The circle was finished. Perfumed smoke drifted across the magical borders as the fire flickered and died.

"O Mighty Eagle," the mole began to incant, "come! Fly hither. Ruler of the forest and the waters, of meadows and moors, of moors and mountains. Come! O one whiter than the sandy shore or the cottony cloud, come, we beg you. Fly from the snowy summit where you dwell, from where you watch the fish devour the fly and the bear devour the fish, from where you watch the flowers blossom in the spring and perish in the fall, from where you see the earth blanketed white with snow in the winter and burst white with blossom in the spring. Come. Come, if you choose to help these goodwilled folk to help another." The mole stood silent then. No one said a word. They listened only, and watched the sky.

"Look! Oh, look!" cried Glister, burrowing into the sand. He stared at the eastern sky. Far away, far away over the cliffs, over the forest came a creature flying with the sun at its back. Its wings were immense and shone like old ivory in the morning sun.

"Oh, dear me," said Mr. Trembly.

"Shiver my timbers," said the Captain.

"By my jewel," said Mirais, taking off his hat and shielding his eyes from the sun to see better. "How far away he must be, yet see how big he is, and look how forcefully he moves his wings."

"I have done it," said the mole. "I, Robertus Magnus, have summoned the mightiest power of all that takes animal form."

When the Eagle's shadow darkened the cliff side, the seagulls, terns, and pipers, feeding where the waves licked the sand, set up a loud shrilling cry and winged out to sea. The Eagle flew steadily in. He covered great distances with each huge sweep of his wings. His dark eye glinted in the sun. His sharp beak held a fixed frown. His tail feathers shone in the sunlight. His lowered talons were terrible to see. The Eagle swept low over the magic circle. He gave a fearful shriek and dove down.

"Down!" cried the Captain, pushing Mr. Trembly and Mirais and the mole into the sand. Wings and air rushed by their ears. They looked up. The Eagle veered high over the sea. He banked in a great wheeling of wings. Then he circled the magic square like a hawk hungry for a mouse.

"He'll kill us!" shouted Glister, poking his head out of the sand. "These circles are no protection." The snake started out of the Inner Circle.

"Stay! Or you'll be done for!" shrieked the mole. He seized the snake.

"Stay," said Mirais, first looking at Glister then anxiously overhead. The snake returned.

The Captain whispered to the toad. "Perhaps we can talk to him," he said.

Just then the Eagle dove at them again. Once again they fell flat, with their noses in the sand. The shriek of the descending Eagle filled their ears. They felt the rush of his wings at their back.

"Help!" cried the mole. "HELP!" They looked up again. The Eagle was carrying off the blind old mole who had dropped the cane and was now kicking and wriggling. The Eagle flew over the sea, dipping the mole's heels in the white wave tops.

"What will he do to him, Mirais?" said the mouse.

"What will he do to *us*?" said the snake.

"Better make for the cave," advised the Captain.

"Look, mouse," said Mirais, "he's bringing him back." The White Eagle was returning. The mole was still in his grasp. A stinging cloud of sand rose as the Eagle alighted.

EIGHTEEN

*In Which the Toad Puts Away
His Polite Tongue and the Mole Is Menaced
with Shadows of His Own Conjuration*

The White Eagle folded his huge wings and released the mole. Mirais got to his feet with the help of his cane and the Captain. Mr. Trembly dusted himself off and took off his glasses to wipe them. The snake poked his head out of the sand where he was again hidden. Even *he* was thinking of the safe home they had left behind. The mole, who was very much shaken, began to speak. "Do not fear," he said, but his teeth rattled so much they could hardly understand him. "I've told the White Eagle why you came to see me and why I dared to summon him with a magic square."

"High Lord," said Mirais, coughing as the dust

settled, "have mercy." The toad held his cap in his hand. The sun sparkled on his green jewel as he spoke. "We ask your pardon and aid." The Eagle glared at the old toad with a wild and fierce look. His beak, Mirais noticed, was exceedingly sharp. "My name is Mirais." The toad stretched his hand towards the Captain. "This is Captain Pelagon." The Captain tipped his sand-dusted hat. Then he remembered to take it off. "This mouse is Mr. Trembly." The mouse bowed low with one arm in front, one in back, as he had learned in Couronne. "This is Glister," said the toad, pointing with his left hand to the cane in his right, for the snake had twisted himself about the tip in the sand. The Eagle said nothing. The mole dared not move. Mirais continued. "We entreat Your Lordship to aid us in returning a little male-child to his natural shape so that his cousin, who has been very kind to us, I must say, will be happy once more."

The Eagle spoke, looking down sharply at the toad. "Mirais, put away your polite tongue. Do you not understand that I knew before you had set out from Innisfree that we should meet on this shore? Do you not see that my very coming is sign of my approval? I am well aware of your own wise wealth"—the sun glinted brightly in the Eagle's hard eye and on Mirais's jewel—"of the snake's youth and eagerness for adventure"—like a green shoot around a bean pole, Glister looked up at the toad, and then turned himself about the cane shyly—"well aware I am of the Cap-

tain's skill and bravery in bringing you here, and of
his love and knowledge of what is around him"—the
Captain shuffled his feet in the sand and gave his
head a quick scratch—"and of the mouse's love for
his house by the Pond, and of his greater love for his
niece." Mr. Trembly's black, little eyes shone behind
his glasses. He twisted his whiskers, and flicked his
tail in a somewhat proud, somewhat nervous, fashion. For he, like the others, was overcome with the
honor of being spoken about by the White Eagle,
whom very few saw, let alone, met. "Well I know,"
continued the Eagle, "why you came to this dealer in
hocus-pocus, in the occult forces, who has done more
good today than in his entire strange life"—the mole
brushed his black gown and thought of the honors
he would claim for summoning the White Eagle—
"this Dr. Polymathus, this Dr. Know-It-All." The mole
frowned, but . . . respectfully. "My presence, as I have
said, is sign of my approval, Mirais. I shall see to the
cousin of Molly, if he has learned his lesson. We must
depart today, for the season is late. The sycamore is
bare. The walnut is bare. The oaks have lost their
leaves. The folk at the Pond and the people of Couronne and Innisfree are already preparing for the winter sleep." The Eagle fixed his cruel eye on the mole.
"Mole, break up your circles that nearly lost you your
life, before they attract more trouble." The mole entered the precincts. Mirais and his friends came out.
"Dance them to dust!" commanded the White Eagle.

With a quickness unbecoming his old age, the mole began breaking the rim of Tetragrammaton with rapid steps of his feet. Mirais remembered how quick, dark and spider-like the mole had seemed when he had played the organ. Robertus held his black arms high and opened the palms of his hands toward the sun. He put his head far back and danced wildly. "By the power of the mighty Adonay, Elohim, Sabaoth, I license thee to depart, spirits, whence thou came!" The mole whirled about, hands high, like a black beetle caught in a watery whirlpool. The four flaps of his gown stood out at his sides as he turned about. He slowed his step and gave the Eagle a quick look. (*He's not really blind*, thought Mirais.) Then the mole hurriedly cried, "Be ready to answer my call when it pleases me." The Eagle frowned harder, but let it go. The mole's feet shattered the Circle of El, the Circle of Yah, the Circle of Agla, and danced into the Circle of Adonay. His feet scourged the Square of the Holy Name in rapid, treading, tramping turns. "Depart!" he screeched in a whirling frenzy. The winds arose. Shadows struck the sand again. The animals cowered as the sand and shadows flew and the wind howled like a hungry bobcat. The Eagle stared unmovingly at the dancing mole who twisted about, shrieking and batting his hands at the air like someone swatting at a swarm of bees. He cupped his hands to his ears and kept on dancing as the wind and sand roared about him in black clouds. Faster and faster, his feet whirled him about. Faster swirled the sand about him. Still he danced. "Weil-away! Be gone. By Sator, Vaol, Shoel, Gashil. Be gone!" he shrieked, holding his ears. But the shadows refused to retreat. Almost hidden, he was, in the cloud of twisting shadows, wind, and sand that raged about. The animals hid under the wings of the Eagle. The mole staggered blindly. Ineffectually.

"Be gone," commanded the Eagle in a low voice. The black storm broke with the sound of many, ugly squeals. One shadow rushed to the sea. One rushed to the cliffs. One rushed to the North. One rushed to the South. The mole dropped unconscious to the sand. The Eagle lifted his wings and let out Mirais and his friends. "Captain Pelagon," said the Eagle, "take Mr. Trembly and see to the magician. Carry him back to his cave."

The Captain gave the Eagle a snappy salute. "Aye," he said, "by Mercury, I'll warrant he'll not call *that* spell again."

The Eagle laughed—rather, he shrieked, for the Eagle found it hard to laugh like other animals. His feathers bright with sunlight, he turned to Mirais. "Go with Glister to the edge of the ocean. There, offshore, you shall find two white pelicans perched on the tops of two wooden pilings. Take the blue rowboat beached there, and go speak with them."

Glister looked curiously at the White Eagle and at the toad.

NINETEEN

Why the Pelicans Perched There and What
the Snake and the Toad Learned from Them

Mirais hopped down the beach toward the water while the snake sidewinded slowly across the difficult sand. They reached the place where the beach was wet with the last reach of the waves and where little stick-legged sandpipers shoveled with their beaks for sand crabs. Broken shells, the strange, many-colored money of the sea, littered the beach. Mirais and Glister were careful not to get cut. Nests of seaweed, salty and dry, were cast up on the shore, nests made by the wind and water, nests, which hatched no bird, but only a brood of heavy smells. Far out, the sea seemed blue; closer in, it was greenish; and when the sun struck the sandbars in the shallows, it was yellow.

Mirais and Glister took off their cloaks in the heat of the late morning. Like an old, smoothed rock or a knobby round of driftwood, Mirais squatted on the white sand where the last finger of the waves wrinkled the shore. Like a streamer of green seaweed freshly cast from the ocean's floor, Glister stretched out next to the toad, letting the water cool his skin.

A tiny blue boat was anchored in the sand farther down the beach. Some gulls were fighting over a starfish near its bow. Not very far from shore were some large rocks, chiseled by the force of the wind, the rain, and the waves into odd mushroom and chimney shapes. Birds flew about the rocks crying loudly to one another. Still farther, but not by much, stood two tall, thick, wave-washed, salt-whitened, and barnacle-encrusted wooden pilings. They were about five feet apart and cocked at odd angles, each not quite straight in the water. Two white pelicans perched atop them. One roosted facing the cliffs; the other looked out to sea. Both sat with their heads pulled into their front feathers, staring blankly.

"Mirais, why did he say to row out there?"

"I don't know. Indeed, I do not know." The toad squinted at the water, for the sun was very bright on the waves.

"Mirais, I feel uneasy about it. Not the way, I mean, I felt uneasy about going underneath the Falls, or about traveling that swamp at night, or about meeting the crow, or the mole, or even the White Eagle."

"Yes, Glister?"

"Well, it's cold during the nights, Mirais, and I would like to go home; yet, seeing that blue boat and those birds just offshore, I'd also like to row out to them. I'd like to hear what they have to say to me."

"I know, Glister, it's adventure. And it's lonesomeness."

"But, Mirais, I feel the same way at once. I can't make heads or tails of anything. One moment I think I'll learn by looking further. We look further and I find just one more riddle, like the owl that Molly said turned into a crow, or that boy who became a tree, or the mole who's blind, yet can see better than I. Mirais?"

"Yes."

"I hardly understood a word King René said, even when he spoke our language."

"Well, Glister, he was a very wise-dealing, yet unexplaining king."

"I always knew he was right, yet I didn't very often know why."

"You're a young snake still."

"I suppose," said Glister, wondering if he'd ever understand why things happened as they did. He and Mirais watched the pelicans.

"Glister?"

"Yes?"

"Old as I am, I understand little of what goes on about me. Just think if I had never climbed Duck Hill back at the Pond. Why, by my jewel, snake, we never would have seen those jays tilting at Mr. Trembly's house, or heard of the hawk who stole Lilac. Glister?"

"Yes?"

"We never would have begun this journey."

The little snake poked his head into a large, empty, pink sea urchin's shell. He pulled his head out as if he had discovered something important inside. "And, Mirais, if we had not met the Captain, we never would have gone to Couronne or to Innisfree. We never would have met Molly. We never would have found Lilac."

"Indeed," said Mirais, looking into the empty shell, too.

"Did the cardinal do all this?" asked Glister. The snake curled into the half of a huge clam shell, but it was too small to hold him.

> *"Good luck is what the cardinal brings,*
> *But eagles rule all earthly things.*
> *Still, sun and moon and stars and seas*
> *Have final power over all that be,"*

said the toad.

"Even over the White Eagle?"

"I suppose. I do suppose, though how or why or when all this came to be is a mystery yet to me, Glister."

"Let's ask the pelicans," said the snake, "they might know." Happily, he wriggled off down the wave-wet beach to the rowboat.

The toad and the snake—the toad rowing, the snake in the bow—quickly got past the rocks. The shallow water invited no large breakers. The pelicans did not even notice them as they moored their boat to the pilings. Mirais let the snake do the talking.

"The White Eagle sent us," shouted up the snake. The two birds looked down, craning their necks awkwardly, turning their heads to one side and staring with their blank eyes at the blue boat bobbing in the water. Then, once more, they turned their gaze to the cliffs and to the water. The snake was annoyed with their lack of response. "Well, who are *you?*" he said. The waves rocked the boat, knocking it against the wooden pilings in an easy rhythm. The birds looked down again.

"I am the Pelican Who Faces the Sea," said the one.

"I am the Pelican Who Faces the Shore," said the other.

—"watching, we are, for seekers," they said in one raspy voice.

—"who have sailed in search," said the one facing the westward sea.

—"who will set sail in search," said the one facing the eastward cliffs.

"But why?" said Glister.

"To find out what they have found," they said in one voice.

"What do you do then?"

"If they search for, or have found, something new," said the pelicans, "we tell the White Eagle."

"Oh," said Glister. "A long time ago, did you see two snakes, a blacksnake and a grass snake? Their names," said Glister, "are Alcor and Mizar. They are," he said, "my uncles."

"Ach! Those two!" said the Pelican Who Faced the Shore. "They rowed away many months ago in search of strange lands and unheard-of things. 'I'm going to Lhasa!' the one would shout. 'I'm off to the Land of Punt,' the other would cry. A regular pair, those two were. Tale-tellers of the fabulous, fortune hunters they were."

"What, what happened to them?" asked the young snake nervously, looking at a big wave on the horizon.

The Pelican Who Faced the Sea looked down. "Their boat," he said, "the very blue one you're riding, drifted in a month later, empty."

A tear grew in one of Glister's green eyes. Then a tear grew in the other. He slipped the mooring line free. Mirais, without a word, pushed off with his cane. "Let's go back, Mirais," said Glister in a very sad tone, a very sorry and stricken tone. "Let's go back to the Pond," he said, and he forgot all about his plan to ask about the stars, the sun, and the moon.

When they returned, the mouse and the Captain and the White Eagle were waiting on the shore. Mirais told them what had happened.

Glister was very tearful and downcast. But suddenly his face brightened. "Perhaps they *are* in Lhasa or in the Land of Punt!" he said. "I'll find my uncles wherever they are, or learn what happened."

"No," said the White Eagle. "They are dead and drowned at sea."

The mouse turned away and looked at the ocean.

The Captain shuffled his feet and coughed.

Mirais turned his cane about.

Instead of crying, Glister looked up bravely. "Mirais, someday, I'll set sail to those places—someday soon."

"The winter is closing in, Glister."

"Yes," said Mr. Trembly, "we must return to the Pond."

"Aye, mate. They're right," said the Captain, slapping his cap on his knee. "But come again some spring. This here tar's got one good run left. I'll make that voyage with ye. And it won't be in a rowboat, but in a right trim and seaworthy ship. The *Water Skeeter* will take us there, wherever be Lhasa or Punt, I'll warrant."

"Will you come, Mirais?"

The toad's eyes twinkled. He rubbed his jewel. "I don't doubt but that I will," said the toad with the emerald jewel, which all toads have. He was an old toad. It was a very large jewel.

TWENTY

Farewell to the Captain, Farewell to Innisfree

"How is the magician?" said the White Eagle to Captain Pelagon.

"He's all right, Cap'n," answered the muskrat. "The mouse and me, we left him a-restin' on his cot. The crow is lookin' after him. But, hang me by the yardarm if he's learned his lesson. Nay, not by a rat's whisker. Calls that one to the crow: 'Fetch me my books, my *Grimoire*. I'll tame those demons yet!' "

"I do believe," said the toad, "that more demons dwell within him than without."

"We have no time for him," said the White Eagle. "Nor is there time to return to the Pond by the

Captain's boat. You must come with me." The four looked at one another. "The Captain will have to sail back alone."

"But, sir . . . ," said Glister. The mouse and the toad looked at the Captain.

"It's best, mate," he said. "If I leave the *Skeeter* here, the snow will fall afore I return. The rigging will rot. What's more, I can't leave her in water for the winter. The ice would crack her hull like an acorn." The Captain wiped his eye with a red-checked kerchief. "I'll miss you, I will"—he dug his pipe out of his pocket and stuffed it full of tobacco with his thick thumb—"but it's best this way." The Captain lit his pipe. He did not look at them.

"Will he be all right?" Mr. Trembly asked the White Eagle.

"He will."

"First I'll lay up at Innisfree to make sure Molly's ready for the winter."

"We shall have passed there by then," said Mirais with a wink, for he was thinking of the little girl and her cousin spending the winter together.

"Aye, mate," said the Captain with a nod and a blue puff from his pipe. "Then it's dry dock for the *Skeeter* at Coq d'Or and dry dock for me at *La Cheminée du Roi René* with the King and his Queen, Hélène. Why, I'll be washed and starched, starched and pressed, and smelling like arrowroot soap by next spring, by Saint Christopher, I will." Everyone laughed, everyone but the White Eagle, who was scanning the horizon with his fierce eye. "Aye, mates, and I'll be thinkin' of ye. I'll spend the winter by the King's hearth, by Saint Nicholas, telling him of this here run. I'll tell him how I taught the mouse to haul in sail and to steer a straight course, and how I taught the snake to watch with his ears. I'll try that tune of Mirais's on me mandolin, I will, when the chestnuts are roasting by the fire. Aye, mates," said the baggy-trousered, rheumy-eyed old salt with a sniffle, "I'll be thinking of ye."

Mirais and Mr. Trembly shook hands with the Captain. "Many thanks," said the mouse. "Good sailing," said the toad.

"We'll make that trip in the spring, Captain, won't we?" asked Glister.

"Aye, this spring or another. It's a long winter. I'll be looking for ye, though."

"Come. It's time," said the Eagle. The afternoon sun glinted in his eye. "We'll leave the Captain at his boat." Gently, the White Eagle picked them up in his claws. Glister wrapped himself around the spurs of one of the Eagle's legs. He looked like a green Christmas wreath there. The Eagle's white, massive wings beat the air.

"Oh!" cried the mouse. "Oh, dear."

The toad gulped and clutched his cane.

The Captain held onto his cap.

Higher and higher they climbed at a dizzy speed,

until the cliffs were just a ragged dark line by the white beach where the whitecapped waves rushed in, wrinkling the shore.

"Look!" shouted Mr. Trembly. "There's the battlefield." A rusty stain in a blanket of green marked the place.

In a wink they passed over the delta marshes and the narrow channels, inlets, and waterways. "There she be!" said the Captain. He pointed straight below. The Eagle circled, then dove, giving a fearful shriek. The air rushed by their ears, it cut their breath. The green swamp appeared to rush up at them. At the last moment, the Eagle wheeled up and made a gentle landing on the rotted, rickety wharf. He set the Captain free.

"She's all right," the Captain said, looking over his boat. "Ugh. *That's* a sorry sight." He inspected the red-eyed banner with the crossed bones. Rain had made the red paint run. The eye was all bloody. So were the bones. The Eagle beat his wings before anyone could comment or even reply. "Good-bye!" they shouted. "Good-bye!"

"See you . . . ," shouted Glister, but already they were too high to be heard. The Captain, a small dot now on the boat's deck, waved his cap and rang the ship's bell. For a moment, a swirl of last leaves from an oak blotted him out of their sight. When the leaves blew past, he was smaller and far away.

High above the treetops they flew, upriver to Innisfree. Flocks of mergansers and green herons and night herons started up in fear when the terrible shadow of the Eagle crossed their feeding grounds. Sparrow hawks and chicken hawks darted out of their path.

"There's the lake," shouted Mr. Trembly. A patch of blue broke in the sea of green treetops.

"And the island!" said the snake. Flying low to the water, they neared the island. The shore animals scurried for safety under the hemlocks. "There's Molly's cottage, her orchard, and bean rows . . . and honeybee hives."

The Eagle circled the cottage. Below them, far below them they could see the girl grasp something small and run for the house. "It's Lilac," said Mr. Trembly, "that's her new yellow dress—she made it herself." Even clutched in the Eagle's great claws, he was proud of his niece.

The Eagle dove. The sheep in the meadow scattered, bleating as if a wolf were chasing them. In a swoop, the Eagle landed on the grassy roof.

"Molly, come out. It's Mirais." The little girl poked her golden head out of the window. Mirais peered over the edge of the roof. "Up here," he said.

"Oh, dear," she said. "Oh, dear me." Molly stood wide-eyed in her doorway as the Eagle set the toad, the snake, and the mouse down in her yard. Lilac peeked out of her pocket.

The toad hopped proudly, happily, to them. He

gasped a little for breath. It had been quite a flight for a toad who never had been more than a foot from the ground. "We've come to turn a certain willow back into a boy," he proudly announced.

First the little girl said nothing, nor did she even move. "*Really*, Mirais?" she said, folding her hands together beneath her chin. The toad smiled and whirled his cane about his finger. Molly looked at the mouse who nodded his head yes, and very happily, too. She looked at the snake. Glister turned his look up to the White Eagle. Then she understood. "Oh, Mirais!" she said, dancing up and down with glee. "Oh, Mirais!" She danced so hard she nearly shook little Lilac out of her pocket and onto the ground.

"But only *if* he's learned his lesson," said the Eagle firmly.

"Oh, sir," said the little girl, "I am *sure* he has."

"Well, then, child, button up your coat again and show us the way to the willow," said the old toad, polishing his jewel.

Molly, almost running, nearly tripping, led them through the orchard to a meadow brook. The apple trees were bare now; the fruit was picked or fallen. A bare willow leaned over the smooth water, letting slender branches trail over the surface. They could see that once-broken larger limbs had been tenderly bandaged by the little girl. Molly cried when she saw the willow tree weeping by the brook. "The heavy snows," she said, "broke his branches last year. Then rain and sleet froze about him. He was so very cold you could hear his limbs crack and groan. He's been good to birds, sir," Molly said brightly to the White Eagle, who was staring sharply at the willow. "Why, sir—just look, sir—look at all the warblers that have come to make nests in his branches."

The Eagle cast a stern eye toward the little girl. "Is it true what the owl told me?"

Molly suddenly looked very fearful. "Yes," she said, "but he won't ever do anything like that again, I'm sure. Please, sir," she said, tears tumbling down her smooth brown cheeks, "*please* bring him back."

"Hmm-m-m," said the Eagle. Mirais looked at him hopefully. So did Mr. Trembly and Glister, and so did little Lilac.

Just then a hard short whistle was heard overhead. From across the meadow, bobbing though the air, came a bright red bird. It was the cardinal. He landed in the branches of the willow. Like a candle flame, but much, much brighter, much redder, he whistled and fluttered from branch to branch. He paid no attention, it seemed, to the golden-haired little girl with the tear-streaked cheeks; nor to the little mouse in her coat pocket, wearing the yellow dress; nor to the toad with the jeweled forehead and the golden-cock cane; nor to the mouse, pulling nervously at his whiskers; nor to the snake, warmly wrapped in an exceedingly long sweater and not looking very much like a snake at all; nor, did it seem, did he pay any attention to the great White Eagle perched on a stump behind them all. The cardinal whistled sharply three more times, and flew away.

"So be it," said the Eagle. He rose up on his heavy white wings. He flew about the willow once.

Molly twisted a handkerchief nervously in her hands.

He flew about the willow twice.

They all stared.

Then he turned once more around the tree. When he landed the willow slowly began to shake. Slowly, the branches straightened. Slowly they shrank back into the trunk. The trunk pulled away from the water. Two branches became two wooden arms. The roots curled up into toes. The trunk parted into legs. At the top there grew a head. The bark smoothed, as if molded by hands they could not see. Soon there was a face. Soon, instead of a willow tree, there was a little boy in a brown shirt and green trousers. That little boy, as you may well guess, was James, Molly's cousin.

"James! James!" Molly ran to her cousin and hugged him hard. They held each other's hands and danced in a circle. Molly and James laughed very loud. Mr. Trembly and Lilac danced, too. Glister wrapped his tail about his head and did a somersault, turning like a wheel. Mirais smiled happily.

"James," commanded the Eagle. They all stopped.

"Will you ever harm either animals of the earth, or fish of the water, or birds of the air again?"

"No, sir," said the little boy with the blond hair and the blue eyes. "Never."

"It is well, then," said the Eagle, rising in the air. "Mirais, have everyone ready at morning. Dress warmly. Tomorrow we return to the Pond."

"Yes, sir," said the toad. "Yes, indeed." The Eagle spread his white wings and flew out of sight into the eye of the sun.

TWENTY-ONE

Our Tale Is Ended

That morning there was ice in the water pail and frost on the ground. After they had some tea and some toast, some biscuits of barley bread and some cold goat's milk, they readied themselves for the long journey to the Pond.

"Dress warmly," said Mr. Trembly to Lilac.

"You, too," said James, holding a woolen sweater for the mouse to put on.

"My tail's *numb* with cold, Mirais," complained the little snake.

"My cousins must already be asleep for the winter," said the toad with a thoughtful look.

"Molly," said James, "we must make some bird feeders for the chickadees and juncos, you know. It's getting cold."

"Yes," she said, "and we must cover the flower beds with leaves so their roots won't freeze. Oh!"

A shriek on the roof told them the Eagle had returned.

"He's here. We must go!" shouted Mirais, all in a dither to get everyone going. "Lilac, don't forget your muffler," he said as he hurried the two mice and the snake (who was three times as fat with sweaters and scarves). "Good-bye, child. Look for the Captain. He'll be in today. Good luck, young man."

"Good-bye, Mirais," said the two. "Thank you very much." The little boy bent down and shook the toad's hand in a very manly manner. They opened the door to a dark, gray day.

The Eagle flew down to the yard. With a surprising gentleness he picked them up in his fierce claws. Then he started up with a noiseless, giant beat of his wings.

"Good-bye, Lilac!"

"Good-bye."

"Good-bye, sir," shouted the cousins, looking up at the Eagle above their cottage. They cupped their hands to their mouths and shouted. "Thank you! Thank you!"

"Good-bye. Good-bye."

The Eagle climbed high above the house. The little girl and the little boy waved from the doorway, becoming small as birds to those who were clutched below the Eagle's breast. Soon the Eagle carried them over the water.

It was cloudy and very cold that day. They crossed the lake and flew upriver. Below, all the trees were bare. The forest floor was brown. Most of the birds, they could see, had flown south. A storm appeared to be brewing. After an hour they were very cold. They snuggled closer to the Eagle. The Eagle's strong wings carried them on steadily.

"Look! Look! There's Couronne," said the snake. "There's Coq d'Or." A straight line of thatched houses appeared in a clearing by the River. Smoke quietly strayed upward from their chimneys. The fields were brown and bare and empty. The Eagle swooped low.

"There's the mill house," said the toad. They saw the mill wheel slowly turning, and the high porch. Soon the sleepy village—the tended and trim capital of Couronne—was left far behind.

"Look!" said Mr. Trembly a moment later. "There's the Falls."

"There are no bears fishing now, I bet," said the snake.

"Nor any boats shooting that dark tunnel," said the toad.

On and on they flew. When they saw the little stream that ran from the forest into the River, they banked toward it. Suddenly it began to snow. Swiftly, heavily, in thick wet flakes, the snow drove straight at them. The four tucked themselves into their warm clothes. Kindly, and without a word, the Eagle tucked them up close to his warm feathers. The snow dotted their clothes and fur white, and it covered the Eagle's snow-white wings. Dizzily, the flakes rushed by them. Below, the earth was turning white.

"I see it!" shouted the mouse.

"I do, too!" said little Lilac. "There's the Pond!"

And there it was, nestled in the whitening woods, bare, its water blotted with cakes and patches of snow and ice.

"There's Duck Hill," said the mouse. "Look, it's all white."

"There's my log," said the toad. "It looks like an icicle."

The Eagle landed on Duck Hill. The snow fell gently about them. The Pond was hushed with the first snow of winter. Not a soul was about.

"Where are they all?" said Glister, shaking himself free of a cloak of wet snow.

The toad brushed himself. "Asleep," he said. Snow hung heavy on branches, bending them low. Mirais cupped his hands to his mouth. "HALLO-O-O!" he shouted.

A squirrel poked its gray head out of a hole in the old oak. "Why, bless my soul," he said. "It's Mirais . . . and Mr. Trembly, Glister . . . and, by golly, little Lilac, and . . ." At the sight of the White Eagle shaking his wings, the squirrel jumped back into his hole.

High above them in a snow-laden elm, a blue jay rustled its feathers. Its sleepy eye looked down at the tumble of snow caused by its stir, falling from twig to twig. The snow fell at Mr. Trembly's feet. The jay saw them, screeched in surprise, and flew away to wake the pondfolk.

The Eagle flew up to the top of the old oak. "Mirais," he called down, fixing his hard, dark eye on the toad. "Your tale is a worthy one. A hawk began it by stealing Lilac. And it shall be a hawk that I appoint to tell your tale. He shall tell it everywhere. Even the stars will know the story of your quest, my friends." Mirais bowed his jeweled head. "Fare thee well,"cried the Eagle. With a shriek that brought many a furry head out of a snow-choked door, the Eagle flew away into the howling storm.

"They're all awake and coming," shouted the snake. Down Duck Hill he tumbled in the snow to meet the pondfolk. Mr. Trembly and Lilac slid down after him. What a stir of cries!

Mirais stood alone on the hill overlooking the snow-swept Pond. The snow continued to fall gently, thickly, heavily. Mirais shivered a bit, for he ached in the joints. He thought of the Captain and his mandolin, of King René and Queen Hélène, of Molly and James, of the blind old mole in his lonely cave by the sea, and he thought of the long winter ahead. "Ah," he sighed, "indeed." He tested the snow with his cane. "I've brought them home safe, at last. Yes, indeed," he said softly to himself, "safe, at last."

147